The Realist

The Vers Podcast #3

by
RILEY HART

Copyright © 2023 by Riley Hart
Print Edition

All rights reserved.

No part of this book may be used, reproduced, or transmitted in any form or by any means, electronic or mechanical, including photocopying, recording, or by any information storage and retrieval systems, without prior written permission of the author, except where permitted by law.

Published by:
Riley Hart

This book is a work of fiction. Names, characters, places, and incidents are products of the author's imagination or are used fictitiously. Any similarity to actual persons, living or dead, is coincidental and not intended by the author.

All products/brand names/trademarks mentioned are registered trademarks of their respective holders/companies.

Cover Photography by Kevin D. Hoover
Cover Design by Cate Ashwood
Edited by Keren Reed Editing and Karen Meeus
Proofread by Judy's Proofreading and Lyrical Lines Proofreading

Marcus

To listeners of *The Vers*, a queer podcast I host with my three best friends, I'm known as The Realist—I accept life the way it is, believe in honesty over sugarcoating, and okay, I can maybe be a little bossy.

If you asked *The Vers* guys, they'd tell you I'm a caretaker who's always thinking of others, but they also give over-the-top hugs and don't believe me when I say feelings are the worst.

It's why I have no business offering Kai Lewis a place to stay when he's in need. He's a flirt who makes no secret about wanting in my bed…somewhere I'd like to have him if he wasn't the employee of one of my closest friends. But he's too trusting and leaps before he thinks, so at least he won't get taken advantage of if he's with me.

Now he's always around, wearing shorts that leave nothing to the imagination and saying he wants to take care of me because I'm always doing it for others. It's not long before I can't resist him—a man who likes listening in the bedroom but is stubborn in other situations.

Kai is sweet and funny and gets me to open up to him. Maybe this whole relationship thing wouldn't be so bad…if he wasn't nine years younger…and leaving Southern California soon…or if I had any idea what I was doing.

The Realist *is an age-gap, forced-proximity romance with a bossy realist and a sunshiny flirt who has Marcus wrapped around his finger.*

Chapter One
Marcus

"WHAT ARE WE going to do today?" asked Corbin, one of my three best friends. He'd shown up at my house a little while ago. I needed to edit and master the latest episode of *The Vers*, the queer podcast we hosted with Parker and Declan, the other two from our group of four.

"Nothing. I'm going for a jog on the beach, and then I'll clean up and do some work."

The argument was coming, they always did, so I wasn't surprised when he said, "You've already conquered the residential and commercial real estate markets in Los Angeles County. I think you can take an afternoon off to give me attention."

I chuckled. "So it's all about you, huh?"

Corbin's brows pinched together as if he was confused. "Isn't it always?"

I rolled my eyes before wrapping an arm around his shoulders and kissing his temple. "You're a fuckin' mess, kid," I teased.

He was, but he also wasn't. People who didn't know Corbin well thought his comments came from a place of conceit, but they didn't. Corbin was always looking for something to make him feel better about himself, even when he didn't realize it.

"I have time for lunch before I get back to work," I told Corbin. "What do you want?" I opened the fridge.

"Nah, I'm good. I'm not hungry." When I turned and cocked a brow at him, he sighed. "Ugh. You're so fucking bossy. How about something small, like a smoothie?"

"Perfect. I love chicken Caesar wraps. That was a great idea."

He sat on a barstool at the kitchen counter while I started making our lunch, but he didn't argue.

For most of our lives, it had been me, Corb, Parker, and Declan all here together, but the previous year Dec had fallen in love with Sebastian Cole, a fucking movie star, of all things. For someone labeled The Loner on our podcast, that had come as a shock to most of us. And now Sebastian had just gotten back from promoting his last movie, so they were spending time together, just the two of them.

Then Parker had married and fallen in love with Elliott—in that order. They were planning a second ceremony for next summer.

The point being, they were around a little less, and while Corb would never say it, he was struggling with it.

"No date tonight?" I asked, sliding his plate over to him. *Date* probably wasn't the best word for it. Corb liked sex and hooking up as often as he could.

"Nah, don't think so. I'd much rather bug you." He immediately bit into his wrap. I knew he was hungry.

"You're good at it."

"I know. Just like I know you love it more than you're willing to admit. I bet you end every night with a silent prayer thanking the universe for having me in your life, like…*Gay gods…whoever you are. Thank you for Corbin. He's funny and charming and, really, the best of our group of friends. Do you think I could be more like him?*"

I laughed because how could I not? "You're a fool."

"*You're* a fool," he taunted.

I really did have shit to do, and I was supposed to have dinner with my folks tonight, but I could tell that Corbin didn't want to be alone, so when we finished eating, I said, "Come on. You can help me get the episode finished. I had a busy-ass week, and it should have been done days ago."

"You know you're not the only one of us who can do this. You don't have to take it on yourself every week."

"Do you know me at all?"

"You're a workaholic who loves control. Why do you think I call you Daddy Marcus?"

"Because you like to annoy the shit out of me, remember?"

"Well, that too."

We worked together on getting the episode ready to go live. Our studio was in my house, and while the other guys could help, the studio being here was one of the reasons it made it easier for me to take care of it all... But yeah, I probably wouldn't give up control regardless. Life was a whole lot easier when you took care of shit yourself and didn't depend on others.

Just as we finished, my cell rang. As soon as I saw *Mom* on the screen, I knew what it was about. I was in my midthirties. At my age, this shit wasn't new. I also knew better than to let it get to me. This was life, so why spend time wishing it were something else?

Corbin watched me from across the table as I answered. "Hey, you," I said to my mom.

"Hey, baby. Listen, I know we were supposed to have dinner tonight, but something came up at work. Your dad and I have to put together a proposal for a potential client that could be huge for us." *You're already the top architectural firm in the state. You have people working for you who can do the proposal.* But then, if it were me, I wouldn't trust anyone else to do it either.

"No problem. We'll meet up another day." We lived half an hour away from each other but still seldom got together. Work was always the most important thing in the Alston family.

"Thanks, Marcus. Love you."

She ended the call. I tossed my phone on the table.

"We should go out to dinner tonight," Corbin said. "My treat. Don't argue."

And while Corb had come today so he wouldn't be alone, he'd suggested dinner because he could tell my folks had canceled on me. He would never admit that was the reason, but we both knew it was. "Yeah, but you have bad taste."

He mock-gasped. "I can't believe you just said that to me. I have the best taste." Corbin grabbed my wrist and tugged. "Go shower and get dressed. It's too early for dinner, but we'll make an afternoon of it. I'm sure I can figure out some other shit for us to do. Ooh, we should go to Dec's bar tonight!"

I grumbled but didn't argue. I spent most of my time grumbling at my best friends, but there was nothing I wouldn't do for them, and I was more thankful for them than they would ever know.

Chapter Two
Kai

"How you doin', baby?" Mama asked. We were sitting in my parents' backyard, watching my nieces and nephews play. I'd come to their house the day before for my brother's birthday. I was the only one in my immediate family who'd left Riverside, and though I'd only moved to Santa Monica, they were always telling me they wished I were closer.

"All right. I gotta head back soon. I work tonight."

"I know. I still hate that you're so far away."

"Mama…it's only an hour and forty-five minutes."

She cocked a brow. "I don't care. That don't count traffic, and it's still too far."

I was the baby, and my two older siblings—Jalen and Faith—were always talking shit about Mom spoiling me. I couldn't help it if my mama had good taste. "I know. I miss you too." I hadn't yet told her there was a very real possibility I'd have to move back home soon. Our landlord had jacked up the rent in our apartment, and my roommate—who made a lot more than me and paid more rent for the master bedroom—was moving to San Diego. Rents in Santa Monica were outrageous, and though my boss, Declan, paid me well at the bar, no way could I afford to live there alone. Hell, with the payment spike, it'd be hard to make it even with another roommate, unless I got into a similar situation as I was in now.

But as much as I loved my family and as close as we were, I didn't want to live in the IE—the Inland Empire. I wanted to be in Los Angeles County.

"You listening to me?" Mama swatted my thigh.

"Ouch. Why you gotta be so mean? And sorry, I missed what you said."

"I asked if you're seeing anyone. You're twenty-six and never brought a boy home."

Not everyone had it as good as me with supportive parents, and while I was thankful for that, it was a little hard to explain to her that I had no intention of settling down right now. I was young, queer, and fabulous. I could do that real-life shit later. "That's because I never found anyone worthy of meeting you." Yeah, I was charming my own mama, but what I'd said was true.

"Uncle Kai! Come play with us!" my niece called.

Mama nodded for me to go, and I shoved to my feet. "Yes, ma'am!" I teased, wanting to hang out with Aaliyah but also to escape this conversation.

I spent about an hour with them, Jalen and Faith eventually coming out too. My siblings were both straight and married. Faith was a nurse, Jalen an electrician, and then there was little old queer me, a bartender simply because it was a job. I enjoyed it, but it wasn't my dream—not that I had any idea what my dream was.

Jalen was the first person I'd told I was gay. He'd just hugged me, said it was cool, then taught me how to fight so I could always stick up for myself. I was around ten at the time. At twelve, Faith started giving me manicure lessons when I'd watch her put polish on. Depending on whether you were an asshole or not, I could paint your nails or kick your ass with the best of them. But the point was, being myself had never been an issue for me. Lately, however, I'd been wondering if I should be doing more with my life, like they did. Or at least to avoid putting myself in a situation where I might have to move home because I couldn't afford to live on my own.

★ ★ ★

MAMA WAS RIGHT. Traffic fucking sucked, and it took me longer to get back to Santa Monica than it should. I had just enough time to go home, shower, and get dressed before heading to Driftwood for work. The bar had always stayed pretty busy, but none of us could pretend it hadn't picked up since Declan got outed as being in a relationship with *the* Sebastian Cole. He'd had to hire security, and people definitely came in hoping to catch sight of Sebastian or to hit on the man who was boning him. Sebastian liked to hang out sometimes and be with Dec while he worked, so they'd arranged a little spot for him behind the counter where he was out of the way and people couldn't get to him.

I went in the back door, which I had a key for. Pop music beat through the walls, muffled but still loud. I smiled because I knew it wasn't Declan's thing, but he also understood his target demographic and what they listened to.

Declan was behind the bar, making a drink. We weren't too crazy-busy yet, but it wouldn't be too long before the space got crowded.

"Hey, handsome," I said to Dec, leaning against the bar. He wore a white Driftwood tee that stretched across his chest, similar to how mine was, though I'd cut half of mine off and made it a crop.

"Flirt."

I'd been calling him handsome since not long after I

started working here. He and Sebastian both knew it was all in fun. I liked to flirt. It was kinda my thing.

Declan finished what he was doing, and when the customer slipped away, he turned to me. "Hi. Any news on the apartment?"

Declan was a good boss. There was no doubt in my mind he was asking because he was worried about me and not just because he didn't want to lose me at the bar. "Nah, but I'll figure it out. If not, it won't be the end of the world to move back home."

The heaviness in my chest said it was, though. I loved it here. I wanted to be able to stay out as late as I wanted, fuck whom I wanted, and not be the baby brother who didn't have his shit together.

"I'm keeping an eye out. The guys are too. Sebastian said you can stay—"

I held up my hand. "I appreciate that, but you're my boss. I can't move in with you and your boyfriend…unless you're looking for a third…then maybe." He rolled his eyes, and I winked. "I'll be fine. I bet it's good to have him back."

Declan would've never said the words out loud, but it had been clear how much he'd missed Sebastian while he was gone. He'd been back for a week or so now, and every night Dec was here, Bastian came in at some point too.

I wasn't surprised when he steered the conversation back to work instead of answering. "Eliza will work tonight too. I'll keep her and Jet behind the bar with me. You and the other guys can work the floor."

"Sounds good. The customers love me," I teased.

"That's because you talk so damn much," he joked…well, kinda joked. I did talk a lot.

"Life is too short not to have fun, Declan. You should try it sometime."

"You do remember I'm your boss?"

"Boss, shmoss." I sauntered away, knowing Declan was likely shaking his head at me.

I got to work, making my way around the bar and taking orders. A group of guys in the corner kept trying to get my attention, so I went over to them. "You boys looking for me?" I flirted before seeing a set of blue eyes that looked slightly familiar. "Hey…I think I know you."

He clutched his heart. "You're killing me here."

I didn't know what it was about that sentence that made the pieces fall into place. "Oh shit. Sorry! Ricky, right?" I'd met him on an app, and we hooked up once. Honestly, he'd been kind of a dick, but not too bad, just bossy in a way that hadn't been sexy when normally I ate that shit up. I liked it on my terms, though.

He laughed. "See, I knew you'd remember me. How you been?"

"Good. You?"

We bullshitted for a few minutes. He was charming and funny and, well, hot. And he was clearly interested in a repeat performance.

"You busy tonight?" he asked. When I cocked a brow, he added, "I meant after work."

"I don't know. Maybe, maybe not. We'll see if you get lucky." His friends laughed. "I need to get back to it. What can I get you, baby?"

"You," he replied.

"I said maybe."

They laughed again, and Ricky gave me a flirty smile. "I want you."

"Doesn't everyone? Now order a drink before you lose your chance."

He groaned playfully but then did. I grinned and walked away.

I'd only made it a few steps when my gaze snagged on a guy who was hands down the finest man I'd ever seen—tall, with beautiful brown skin that matched mine, and firm muscles that were definitely bigger than my own. I really wanted to lick…and maybe bite into them. Marcus kept his black hair buzzed short like I did. And I knew his eyes were a whiskey color and almost always serious.

He was one of Declan's close friends, and while I just playfully flirted with Declan and Sebastian, I wanted Marcus. Badly.

My smile grew. This night was turning out to be a good one.

Chapter Three
Marcus

CORBIN HAD DRAGGED me around LA most of the afternoon. We'd had a late dinner in WeHo before heading back to Santa Monica and Declan's bar.

It was still fairly early for being out, only about ten thirty, but Driftwood was already packed. I was proud of Declan for what he'd created here. He liked to put it on me because I'd bought the bar and then sold it to him, but that was just money. It wasn't what made Driftwood a safe space for queer people. It wasn't what made people choose to spend time here rather than going into LA. That was all Dec.

Declan slid a beer to Corbin, then me. I took a swallow, savoring the bitter taste.

"This is a surprise," Dec said.

"Marcus was on my ass all day to hang out. I finally gave in."

I cocked a brow at Corbin, who gave me a grin and nudged me. This fucking kid.

"Hey, baby," came from behind me. I didn't have to turn around to know who it was. I'd recognize Kai's sexy, flirty voice anywhere. I'd be lying if I said it didn't land in my cock. Something about him always went straight to my head—other than his looks, I meant. Part of it was definitely his confidence, the fact that he said what he felt and wasn't shy about what he desired. Too bad I didn't fuck friends...or friends of friends, which meant I wasn't fucking Declan's employee.

"What's up?" I asked before taking a drink. When I finally turned to look at him, I knew it was a mistake. Kai's eyes were darker than mine, a rich mahogany. They were always taking the world in, didn't look at it with the pessimism or caution mine did. They were wide, bright, and damned if I didn't like the feel of them on me.

He was smaller than me—not totally a twink but closer to that than anything else. His mouth was to die for, lips that were made for sucking cock. He kept short, neatly trimmed scruff around his mouth that just drew my attention to it even more. There wasn't a universe in which Kai wasn't fine as fuck, but he was also trouble.

"Eh, it was a good day. Even better now," he replied.

"That so?"

"Yeah, that hot guy over there was flirting with me." He winked, confident little fucker, then turned and walked behind the bar, shaking his ass, clearly for my benefit. It was a great ass, but I had willpower like a motherfucker, so I turned away.

Dec eyed me as if asking a silent question, and I just shrugged. What the fuck could I say? Kai was a flirt, and not just with me. Didn't mean he didn't want to fuck me and that I wouldn't slowly take him apart until he was screaming my name, if it wasn't for the fact that he was too close to home.

"You're determined to put me in an early grave, aren't you?" Declan said as Kai made drinks beside him. While Kai was only seven or eight years younger than us, Declan definitely felt some kind of responsibility to him. He cared about Kai like he would a younger brother, which spoke to Kai's character because Dec didn't get close to just anyone. He was like me that way.

"What'd I do?" Kai asked, batting the dark lashes framing his beautiful eyes.

Declan shook his head as if he didn't know what to do with Kai.

"I get that look all the time, man," Corbin told him. "Don't stress about it."

"Oh, I won't. I'm memorable and make an impression. Isn't that right?" he asked me.

"Kai," Declan warned.

"Someone get Sebastian here. Declan's more chill when he's around," Kai teased, and yeah, Corbin and I both laughed. Kai lit up for a moment, then seemed to be trying to tamp it down like he didn't want us to know how much he'd enjoyed it. A moment later, he headed away with a tray full of drinks.

"That kid wants you," Corbin said.

"He's not a kid," automatically fell from my lips.

My friend frowned. I had a feeling Declan did too, but I didn't let myself look at him. Corbin added, "You call me kid, and we're the same age."

Yeah, I did. I couldn't say why, so I just shrugged.

Declan said, "He's a good kid and a good worker. He worries me sometimes, though."

Curiosity tugged at me. I told myself not to ask, that it was none of my business and I shouldn't concern myself with Kai, but I was suddenly shit at controlling my own damn self. "Why?"

"He's too trusting…doesn't always pay attention to his effect on people, and they tend to want him more than they should sometimes. Guys get handsy with him. We had this man in here for a while who hung around every night he worked, approached him at his car one night. Kai handled it. He can take care of himself, but you know how I get.

Sebastian gives me shit because I kept griping at him for giving me his gate code after we'd been fucking for ten years."

Declan and Sebastian had a secret, no-strings-attached thing going for a long-ass time before the rest of us found out about it, and they actually fell in love. Sebastian would contact Dec when he was in town, and they'd do their thing. It took Declan forever to acknowledge it, but Sebastian had always been special to him.

I turned in my seat, watching as Kai handed glasses to a group in the corner. It was clear he was being flirty with them the way he was with me before heading over to take other orders.

When Declan said, "I need to get to work. I'll be back," I realized I'd been watching Kai like the creeper guys he'd been talking about, so I forced myself to face forward again.

"You like him," Corb said.

"I don't know him."

"You want to fuck him."

"And you wouldn't?" I raised my brows in question.

"Well, yes, but that's beside the point. He calls out to that caretaker nature in here." He tapped my chest, over my heart. I rolled my eyes. They were always saying shit like that to me, but I didn't see it. I liked to help my friends, yeah, but that didn't make me any more special than anyone else.

"There's no doubt in my mind that he can take care of himself," was how I chose to answer, not sure what else to say.

"Taking the easy way out, are we? I see you, Marcus." Corbin grinned. "And that still doesn't mean you don't want to be the one doing it for him. But I'll shut up now before you start calling me on my shit."

I laughed. "Smart man." After taking another drink of my beer, I turned to find Kai again. Damned if the little brat wasn't staring my way…and he winked at me.

I forced myself not to look at him again, something I wasn't used to having to do. I didn't like feeling as if I wasn't completely in control of how I felt or behaved, which meant Kai was a whole lot of fucking trouble.

About half an hour or so later, just as Declan returned to me and Corbin, Kai ducked behind the counter. "Holy shit. I think I just found a place to live," he told Dec, who frowned. "Um...what's that look for?"

"With whom?" Declan asked.

"The guy in the corner. Ricky. We hooked up once. I mentioned looking for an apartment, and he has a room for rent. It's a good price, so I'm going to go look at it with him when I get off tonight. He—"

"You don't know him," I cut him off.

Kai crossed his arms. "Are you slut-shaming me?"

"I wasn't talking about fucking him. I meant moving in with him."

"So? When does anyone really know someone when they rent a room from them? They find a place online, meet, fill out the application, and boom—roommates."

Okay, so maybe the little shit had a point, but still, I didn't like it. I'd always trusted my gut. "I'll look for rentals for you."

He rolled his eyes. "I can't afford much, and I can handle it myself, *Dad*." He leaned over the bar, face close to me. "Daddy is sexy... I can work with that. The other, not so much. Unless you plan on giving me a good reason not to take this offer, it looks like I'm moving in with Ricky. But regardless, what I do is *my* choice." He plucked two beers off the counter and walked away.

"Wait...did he just leave Marcus speechless? I'm pretty sure that just happened, and I've never seen it before," Corbin taunted playfully. The crazy thing was, he wasn't wrong.

"I'm not speechless," I lied.

"Pretty sure you are," Declan countered.

"Stop agreeing with him," I grumbled. We all knew I was full of shit, but I planned to deny the hell out of it as long as I could. "I'm sure you don't like this idea either."

"No, but it makes more sense for me. I know Kai better than you, and I've always worried about him. But ultimately, he's right. He's a grown man who can make his own decisions."

"Wow…that was very adult of you. When did that happen?" The joke rolled right off my tongue, and I hoped it would pull the attention off me and whatever the fuck weirdness I was dealing with. This sure as shit wasn't typical for me. I was the logical one in our group, the realist, and my protectiveness over Kai felt nothing like logic.

Declan said, "You're lucky I'm busy. Otherwise, we'd be having a conversation about why you're trying to change the subject from you to me. Corbin, deal with him." Declan smiled as he walked away.

Corbin opened his mouth, but I cut him off. "I have to take a piss."

"Convenient."

"Want to go with me to make sure I'm really peeing?"

"Is that code for asking if I want to see your dick? Because I love you, Marcus, but you know I don't see you that way."

"You're an idiot." But I loved him too.

Pushing away from the counter, I stood and went to the restroom. Two guys were standing at urinals, another was washing his hands, and someone was definitely fucking in the far bathroom stall.

I stepped up to one of the urinals and had just pulled my dick out and started taking a piss when the door opened behind me, and someone said, "I can't believe you asked that twinky bartender to move in with you."

My gaze snapped up, and I turned to see two of the guys from the corner table walk in.

"Eh...he's a little obnoxious, but I wanted to rent the room out anyway. Money every month and a live-in hole with no commitment. Ain't a bad deal," he replied, which had the two of them laughing.

Anger flared in my chest, an uncontrolled burn scorching my insides. I took a few deep breaths before tucking my cock away. Slowly, with measured steps, I went to the sink to wash my hands.

"Yeah, but what happens when you get sick of him?" the first guy asked.

I dried my hands.

"Then he's gotta go. My house, my rules. Or maybe I'll just change my mind after getting him to my place tonight."

They laughed again, and it took everything in me not to lose my shit. I fucking hated bullies, hated people who didn't care how they treated others.

I waited while they finished pissing. Then the asshole moved toward the sink, and I didn't step out of his way.

"Excuse me," he said, trying to move around me, but I slid to the side, staying in his way. "What the fuck, man?"

"Here's what you're gonna do: wash up and leave. I'll be nice and pay your tab for you, but you're not going to come back here. You're also going to stay the fuck away from Kai. You don't show him your apartment, you don't try to fuck him, you don't hit him up on Grindr. Nothing. You feel me?"

"Fuck you!" he spit out.

"You sure that's how you wanna play this?"

He hesitated, looked at me, then said, "Fine. I don't want him that bad anyway."

One of the other guys in the bathroom laughed, but I just

watched the bully, gaze still on him even when I stepped out of the way so they could wash their hands. I went out of the bathroom when they did, joining Corbin at the counter but not sitting as I watched the guy say something to his friends. Him and his buddy from the restroom turned to look at me before the two of them left the bar.

"What the fuck was that?" Corbin asked.

"Heard some shit in the restroom. I took care of it," I told him, then to Declan, "you don't want them here again. They come back, have security deal with it or tell me." Declan nodded, not needing me to tell him what happened to trust me. "I got his bill. I'll be right back."

Kai was at the opposite end of the bar, passing drinks out. He clearly hadn't noticed what had gone down. When he turned, he took a step and nearly ran into my chest.

"Is there something I can do for you, Marcus? If you're curious, I'm on the menu."

I ignored my cock, which had chubbed up at that. "Yeah, you're moving in with me." Without another word, I turned and walked away.

Chapter Four

Kai

"EXCUSE ME, WHAT?" I stepped along behind Marcus, but he kept going. I grabbed his arm when he had just about reached Corbin, twisting him around and making him bump into me. "Did you miss the part earlier where I said I get to decide what I do? Who said you can order me around?"

He sighed as if I were the one being unreasonable. "Are you telling me you don't want to move in with me?"

Well, of fucking course I did. I wasn't an idiot. "That's beside the point."

"Why?"

Hmm, why was it? Oh yeah. "Because you're not the fucking boss of me!" But then, there were also times I wouldn't mind that, and times I'd *want* it, so I amended, "Unless it has to do with sex. But you pretend you don't want to fuck me, so we're not screwing, which means no telling me what to do, and it would only be *sometimes* with sex, but—"

"Could the two of you do this somewhere else?" Declan asked, his voice raised so we could hear him. When I glanced around, people were watching us. Ricky was gone, I'd noticed, which made my annoyance spike to whole new levels.

"Did you say something to him?" I growled just as Corbin said, "Are you kidding, Dec? If you send them away, we'll miss the show. No one talks to Marcus like this."

Marcus turned to his friend. "Corb, you're not helping."

"Yeah, well, I do," I added. It didn't matter how sexy Marcus was; he didn't get to make my choices for me.

Marcus ran a hand over his buzzed head. "Why are you arguing with me about something that will benefit you? Something you want."

Okay, so there was a small chance he had a point, but still, I was standing my ground. "Because you don't get to make decisions for me. You sure as shit don't get to scare men away from me, if that's what you did. You want me to move in, you can ask." I poked a finger in his chest. "And until you do, the answer is no. I don't care if I have to go back to Riverside instead."

My brain was telling me to shut the fuck up, and when I started walking away, I had to suppress the urge to turn around and go back and talk to Marcus. I heard him say, "Jesus fucking Christ," as if putting all the blame for this on me. I couldn't pretend I didn't want to jump at the opportunity. Stay with Marcus? Fuck yes. But I wasn't going to let him think he had to save me.

"Kai," Declan said when I was behind the bar again.

"What do you want, handsome?"

"He's trying to be nice."

I turned my gaze to Marcus. "Well, he sucks at it."

Something I couldn't read flared in Marcus's gaze just as Corbin doubled over laughing. I watched when Marcus came around the counter as if he owned the place, and then— "What the hell?" I said as he picked me up, tossed me over his shoulder, and began carrying me toward the back of the bar. "Put me down!" There was no heat, no real want behind my words, though I tried to make it sound like there was. This shouldn't be hot, but it was. When a fine-ass man like Marcus Alston tossed you over his shoulder and carried you away like you weighed nothing, it was hard not to let all sorts of sexy fantasies play through your head.

In my mind, he was taking me to Declan's office to bend me over the desk and fuck me—and I was correct about the place, only when we got there and I went to pull my shirt off, he asked, "What are you doing?"

"Oh, we're not having sex?"

"Jesus," he said again, scratching the back of his neck. "You don't even know that guy."

"Have a good night." I went for the door, but he groaned and wrapped his hand around my wrist. "We already went over this, Marcus. How many times do I have to explain how renting a room works?"

"Has anyone ever told you you're a stubborn little thing?"

"What do you think?" I tugged out of his hold and crossed my arms. "I have a job to do, so if we're finished here, I would appreciate it if you didn't go all caveman on me every time I try to walk away from you. I also have to get ahold of Ricky somehow…you know, so I have a place to live." There was a good chance Marcus hadn't said anything to him. I wasn't naive. I knew Ricky was a dickhead. He could have been blowing smoke up my ass and had no intention to rent me a room, but I needed to find out.

Marcus sighed. "Would you like to rent a room from me?" he asked, his voice even and tight.

Oh, wow…I hadn't really thought he would utter the question. If he hadn't, I would have regretted my behavior later because staying with him sounded like a dream come true, but I didn't ever want people to think they could take advantage of me. If I let someone make decisions for me because sometimes it *was* hot, it would only happen on my terms.

"I appreciate your asking, but no, thanks," I replied, and

watched as his pupils blew wide. A second later he'd recovered and could clearly tell I was giving him shit.

"You're the most annoying person I've ever met."

"Thank you, and yes, I would love to rent a room from you. How much?"

"We'll figure that out later, but it'll be something you can afford."

I had a feeling it would be less than the room was worth, which made me feel slightly guilty for how I'd reacted, but then I remembered it felt sorta like foreplay, so go me. "It has to be fair."

He frowned. "I would never take advantage of you."

"I meant fair to *you*, Marcus." That seemed to shake him, as if he hadn't expected it.

"Give me your cell number. I'll text you tomorrow." He tugged his phone out and typed my info in. My phone buzzed against my ass with what was likely a text from him so I had his number.

It seemed to zap a dose of reality into me, and it struck me what was happening here. Marcus was renting me a room...not because he needed or wanted a roommate. In fact, there was no doubt in my mind it was completely the opposite. He was doing it because I was in need and he cared about people. Though he would never admit it, he liked helping. He loved being able to swoop in and save the day, and I couldn't help wondering if anyone ever saved the day for him. Declan, Parker, and Corbin, I was sure, but anyone else?

"I'm sorry for acting the fool. You were being kind to me, and while I stand by what I said, that neither you nor anyone else gets to tell me what to do, I appreciate where you were coming from, and this...what you're doing...means a lot to me. You won't regret it."

"Oh, I'm sure I will," he responded with a deep chuckle,

but then... Was it me, or was Marcus closer?

"You won't regret it *much*," I amended.

A wave of shivers started in my neck and flowed down the length of my body when he hooked his finger beneath my chin and tilted my head up. "You're going to test me."

"Yes." Why lie? We both knew it was true, and I was pretty fucking sure we both wanted it. For whatever reason, Marcus was just being stubborn.

He rubbed a thumb over my bottom lip. I sucked in a sharp breath before getting myself under control. I sneaked my tongue out and licked it. I moaned when Marcus pushed the digit into my mouth, and then I began to suck. Goddamn, I wanted him so fucking much. When he pulled it out, I tried to bite him, but Marcus's hand was too quick. "That was hot, Marcus."

"Yes. Too bad we're going to live together. It's just another reason I can't have you."

I was frozen, my feet suddenly cemented to the floor. It took a moment for his words to click, and by the time they did, Marcus was already stepping around me and heading for the door. He'd just pulled it open when I said, "Wait. Why?"

He didn't answer, just kept walking, and damned if I didn't follow him like a lost puppy. "But you really do want me too? Because that's a pretty important piece of information. I might be willing to live in the streets to make that happen."

He chuckled, then slowed down so I could catch up. "Too late now. No fucking if you do or don't move in."

"Well, considering I didn't know it was actually on the table before I agreed to move in, I'm objecting."

Marcus cocked a brow. "Overruled."

I sighed as we continued down the hallway. "You like to torture me, don't you?"

Marcus looked at me, his intense gaze like a caress against my skin. "I can promise you, baby boy, you torture me even more."

With that, he exited the door and made his way back into the main part of the bar. "Wait! Then why say no? Why do we have to deny ourselves?" I asked, again chasing after him. I had a feeling that was going to be my MO from now on because something about Marcus Alston got to me. I'd never wanted anything as much as I wanted him, and if he felt the same, I damn sure planned to have him.

Chapter Five
Marcus

"HELLO AND WELCOME to *The Vers*, where four friends who rarely agree on anything share their versatile opinions about everything. I'm Corbin Erickson, The Charmer."

"Marcus Alston, The Realist."

"Parker Hansley-Weaver, The Romantic."

"Declan Burns, The Loner," Dec finished just as Corbin began speaking again.

"Hey! I didn't interrupt Declan this time." Corbin cheered, and the rest of us rolled our eyes.

Parker jumped right into the show. "Good job, Corb. I think we should all do a random check-in, and let's start with…hmm…maybe Marcus? What's new in your life?"

Fuck. Because of course Declan or Corbin would have told him what happened. I was actually surprised it was Parker who mentioned it. "Nothing to tell," I replied.

Corbin said, "So we're not going to talk about how a sexy little twink got you to not only allow him to live with you, but also for you to *ask* him to do it? Nah, that's not gonna fly." Corbin gave me a playful grin, and goddamn it, what had I been thinking telling him the whole story? I'd just been so…well, fuck, *shocked* that it had happened in the first place that as soon as Corbin and I left the bar, I'd spilled the whole thing. I couldn't wrap my head around the fact that Kai had been able to get me to do that. It was completely out of character for me. Maybe I would've done that shit with the men in this room with me, but not with anyone else.

"We're editing this out," I said.

"You're no fun," Parker said. "The rest of us are always getting our shit put on blast. It's your turn."

"Yeah, well. That's different." As far as excuses went, it was a weak one, but it was all I could come up with. "Can we do the show, please?"

"Not sure if you think we're solving world hunger here, but this *is* the show," Dec said. "This is literally what we do every week—talk shit and annoy each other."

"Eh, do what you know." Corbin shrugged. "We're good at it."

Parker said, "Can we talk about Marcus having a roommate now? I think it's sweet and one of the most Marcus things he could do." He gave me a supportive smile as if that comment had been doing me a favor.

"The most Marcus thing Marcus could do?" Corbin asked, but I spoke before Parker could reply.

"Nope. Don't even think about it. I know you, Park. I can see the story writing itself in that spark of fantasy in your eyes. Fiction isn't real life."

"Well...I mean, for me and Dec it has been."

"Should I go into the percentage of relationships that don't work out? How many marriages end in divorce? And of the ones that don't, I wonder what's the actual percentage of happy people. Most of the time they stay together because it's easy, comfortable, or for financial reasons."

"Wow, talk about a downer," Corbin chastised, and he had a point. I was such an asshole sometimes.

"Shit. Sorry. Not for you guys. I just... Why are we even

talking about this?"

They were all quiet for a second. Nerves itched at the base of my neck, making me wonder how much I'd fucked up. I believed in Declan and Sebastian—and in Parker and Elliott. Me? I was married to my work, just like my parents...well, and to the three people in this room. Romance and attraction were mostly chemical reactions people decided to make last long-term, and in my brain, that just didn't compute.

"Who thinks Marcus needs a hug?" Corbin asked, breaking the tension. There was an extra beat of silence before we all dissolved into laughter, and it was this right here, this moment, that I needed. While I was happy for Parker and Declan, it was the three people in this room I trusted, who would never let me down and would always make time for me and *want* to spend time with me. The other shit was just what society told us we should want. It was a lie they sold us that didn't fit everyone's life. That didn't fit me.

When everyone settled down, I said, "Okay, let's jump into some listener questions."

I glanced at Corbin, who began scrolling on our tablet. "Oh, this is a good one. I'm not sure how qualified we are to answer..."

"Are we actually qualified for anything?" Dec asked.

"Good point, but this is a little different because none of us identify this way. I think it's an important discussion, though, so I'll ask and preface it by saying this isn't *own voices* for us, so take our response with a grain of salt. We're not experts. And please, if we get anything wrong, message us, and we'll be sure to discuss it on the next show." He cleared his throat. "*How can I make people understand there's a spectrum when it comes to asexuality? It's not all or nothing.* It's signed 'Searching for Answers.'" Corbin looked at the rest of us as if waiting for us to answer.

When no one spoke, I said, "I think this is similar to a lot of things in life, and there are a lot of shades of gray. Unfortunately, most people look at everything as black or white and ignore that gray areas exist. We don't look at situations and consider nuance. Or we tend to think our experience is the *only* or *right* experience. So unfortunately, I'm not sure we can *make* people understand at all."

"Not helping, Marcus," Parker piped in.

"I wasn't finished. You're acting like Corbin with the interrupting."

"Hey, what did I do?" Corb pouted.

I shook my head. "As I was saying, people have to *want* to listen and open their minds, and we can't make others do that, but the truth is, there isn't one way to be or do anything. I'm a Black man, and while there are similarities and certain things all Black men go through when it comes to society and things like that, all our stories aren't the exact same. My story as a gay, Black man is different from someone else's. There's not one way or one experience, just like there's not one way to be gay, female, Mexican, nonbinary, trans, and so on. The best you can do is know your truth, know who you are and that no one can tell you how to be you. No one can tell you it's wrong." Even when you looked at Kai and me, both of us being gay, Black men didn't mean *all* our experiences were the same. Some? Of course. But no group was a monolith.

"That doesn't mean they won't tell you it's wrong," Declan added.

"Good point. You just have to ignore them." Corbin nodded before Parker jumped in.

"And if you want to explain to people, you can. You shouldn't *have* to make excuses for yourself, but if you'd like to share, you should. Just keep in mind that you shouldn't hold yourself responsible for how much they listen or understand. I have limited experience being married to a man who figures he's likely demiromantic, but again all he can do is tell people it's a spectrum and the rest is up to them."

Corbin said, "It's hard because we all want to relate, right? We want to see ourselves in others, and we want them to see who we are, but no one has our lived experience as *individuals*, so most of the time, they don't get it. It's easy to look at someone and decide who they are and what that means, but that's based on your life experience and preconceived notions." When Corbin finished speaking, I put my arm around him and pulled him close. He came easily.

"As with any group," I continued, "there are a lot of stereotypes out there about ace people. It's up to us to break those down and not make assumptions. Still, it's also up to others to want to hear you. The best you can do is educate as you feel comfortable, without harm to yourself, and leave it in their hands. I know, very *realist* of me, but I don't know how else to put it."

Parker said, "We hear you, though, Searching for Answers. And maybe at some point, we can look into having someone on the show to talk about asexuality. I'm sorry if our answer isn't great. As Dec said, we're not really qualified for any of this." Parker turned to Corbin. "What's the next question?"

We answered a few more, then bantered over a story Parker told about him and Elliott. By that time I'd shared info on our sponsors, and we ended the show. I expected Kai to be mentioned any second now, and Corbin didn't let me down.

"When does your boy move in?"

"Next weekend, and not my boy." He'd called like I'd asked, and we'd figured out the logistics, decided on rent and things like that. I didn't want to charge him at all. What was the point? My mortgage was the same regardless. But Kai wouldn't accept that offer.

I was still trying to wrap my head around having made the offer for him to move in at all. Unlike what Park said, I didn't think it was the most Marcus thing I could do. We were going to annoy the shit out of each other. My home was my space—well, our space, *The Vers*'s—and the thought of having someone else there all the time weighed on me.

"You're freaking out," Corbin told me.

"No I'm not." I bristled. I might call them on their shit, but I didn't like it when people did it to me.

"Yes, you are," Declan added. "But I appreciate your helping him out. Kai is a good kid."

"He's not a kid," I reiterated, and the second I did, it hit me how big a mistake that was. My response was just the opening they needed.

"Who wants to take bets on how long it takes Marcus to bang his new roommate?" Corbin asked.

Fuck my life. "Why am I friends with you guys?"

"You realize Kai is my employee, right? I'm used to having to tell him not to flirt, but do I have to scold you on what's appropriate too, Corbin?"

"Two weeks tops," Parker threw in.

"Jesus Christ. Are you shitting me? What makes you think I'd fuck someone so close to my family?" It was like déjà vu to how many other similar situations between the four of us? Except it was never me in the hot seat.

We stood and left the studio, Corbin right on my heels. "Um…because every time you look at him, you give him that Marcus stare—the growly, seductive, *I want to wreck you until you don't know any other men exist but me.*"

"I don't do that shit." Did I do that?

I went straight to the kitchen. Elliott and Sebastian weren't here today. I was pretty sure they were out having lunch, so I was going to cook something for the four of us.

"Yes you do," Parker said. "How don't you know you do that? It's really fucking hot. I've seen you give that look a million times over the years, but it's even more intense with Kai."

This was followed by Declan's, "I'm stuck between finding this entertaining and being worried. You do want him, Marcus."

I groaned. "No shit. Of course I want to fuck him. Have you seen him? But I have control over myself and I won't because too much can go wrong." I didn't want to risk putting Declan in the middle, or him losing an employee if shit went sideways. And now that Kai was moving in, I really wasn't going to sleep with him. That was the opposite of having the situation under control. It made things messy, and I didn't do messy.

"So…did anyone notice his nipples are pierced?" Corbin asked, and goddamned if heat didn't rush to my groin.

"I'm going to kill you."

He grinned. "If you're not going to sleep with him, do you mind if I see if he wants to hook up? He seems fun."

"No one's fucking Kai," I said, my voice too sharp, like the blade of a knife cutting through what was now a quiet room.

"Well, shit. Daddy Marcus has spoken," Corbin teased.

"Daddy Marcus has staked his claim!" Parker taunted, and the three of them laughed. I stood in front of the open fridge, watching them and knowing I was fucked.

Chapter Six

Kai

I'D SPENT THE whole week packing. The good thing was, I didn't have a lot of furniture. It was mostly just my bedroom stuff, since the apartment was furnished with my roommate's things. I'd lived with him since I moved to Santa Monica. Anders and I weren't close, but it worked for us. I'd been so ready to leave Riverside, it hadn't mattered that I didn't have much. The most important thing I owned was my seventy-five-gallon saltwater fish tank. Luckily, that didn't have to go today. I still had to figure out the best process for moving it and keeping my babies alive.

"We ready to do this?" Anders asked.

"Yep, I—"

Knock, knock, knock.

"You expecting anyone?" I asked.

"Nope."

My Marcus senses started tingling, a prickling at my nape. I didn't know why my thoughts automatically went there, because why the fuck would Marcus be at my apartment? It wasn't as if he knew where I lived... But it wouldn't be hard to find out, and why was I standing here like an idiot instead of seeing who was at the door?

"I'll get it," I told Anders, and sure enough, as soon as I opened it, there he was.

I crossed my arms.

He smiled, which was really hot, but I tried not to focus on that.

"It's cute when you get mad."

"What are you doing here?"

"Helping. I want to make sure I'm around so you don't bang up my walls or anything when you move in."

Which okay, yeah, I could see him being particular about things like that, but there was more to it too. I knew from stuff I'd heard at Driftwood how much Marcus was always putting himself out there, always the one trying to help when his friends needed something. What I couldn't figure out was why he was doing it for me.

"Well, if you think I'm gonna argue, you're wrong. I like watching sexy men lift things."

He snorted, shaking his head, and I stepped aside so he could come in. Anders's tongue was hanging out of his mouth as he took Marcus in. I couldn't blame him. I'd done the same the first time I'd seen him.

"I'm Marcus. You must be Anders." Marcus held his hand out for my roommate—well, ex-roommate. Had I mentioned his name to Marcus before? If so, it had to be in passing, but clearly, he remembered.

"Nice to meet you, Marcus." When Marcus continued into the apartment, Anders whispered, "*That's* who you're moving in with?"

"Yep." I grinned.

Marcus, always to the point, asked, "Where do we start?"

"I just have a few kitchen things. Two boxes on the table. Everything else is in my bedroom, other than the tank. Anders said I could keep it here for a few days until I organize the move. It's going to be difficult to transport. I really don't want to lose any of them."

"This is yours?" His brows drew together as he pointed at the fish tank.

"Don't look so surprised. I can keep things alive. I'm more of a functioning adult than you seem to think."

"That's not what I meant." He walked over and looked at the tank. I had two clownfish, a blue tang, gobies, banggai cardinals, and my reefs, which I was really proud of.

I joined him. "You have to be really careful, especially with the reefs. I'm gonna need to buy every bucket at the hardware store. It took me a long time to get this right, and I'm scared I'm gonna screw something up when I move it."

"Don't they have services for that?"

"I'm sure they do." They probably weren't cheap either.

"I'll look into it. We'd be smart to hire someone."

I quirked a brow. "We would, huh?"

"Protect your investment, Kai. This is a lot of money and time."

"And heart." I tapped his pec. "Don't pretend you don't have one, baby. I see it."

He rolled his eyes. "Stop flirting with me."

"Stop trying to save the day."

"I'm being logical."

"You're being bossy."

"Um…should I leave you two alone? Because you look like you're about to rip each other's clothes off." Anders broke the moment, making me jerk away from Marcus, whom I'd somehow gotten closer to than I'd been a moment before. Fuck. I was simping for his cock too fucking hard.

"Nah, he says we can't have sex. I've tried."

Marcus shook his head, but I was pretty sure he was trying not to smile. "Be good."

"You know hearing you say that turns me on more, right?"

"Really? The person who doesn't want to follow rules or have someone tell him what to do?"

"I said only under certain circumstances and only when I want it." I winked. "Come on, baby. I'll show you to my room. Not for sex, though." Marcus sighed but went with me. "Anders has a truck. I figure we can get everything in two loads. He said he has the whole day to help."

"I rented a moving vehicle, so we can get it in one."

"What the fuck, Marcus! You have to stop doing that shit. How do you know I didn't already do that, and then we'd have two?"

"Declan told me. Stop doing what?" He crossed his arms.

My gaze darted toward Anders. "Nothing. We'll talk about it later."

The truck was a good idea, which I'd of course thought about on my own, but I was trying to save the money. Anders didn't mind helping for free.

The move did go quicker with Marcus there helping and having the larger vehicle to move everything in, and before I knew it, I was driving my car, Marcus the truck, and Anders was waving goodbye since Marcus had told him we could unload by ourselves.

I'd never been to Marcus's house before. I knew it would be nice, but nothing had prepared me for the gorgeous monstrosity of a beachside villa. The place had to be more than five thousand square feet, a white house with an orange-tiled roof, secluded even though there were neighbors close, and with trees and plants surrounding it.

My little Toyota would definitely stand out. The second I got out of the car, I said, "Holy shit. This is where you live?"

This was where *I* lived?

"It's not a big deal."

"Says you. Holy fuck, Marcus. I can't live here with you."

He frowned. "Why?"

Um…I didn't really know. "It feels like taking advantage of you. It's weird. I knew you had bank, but I didn't think you had this." I waved my hand at the fucking mansion. I suddenly felt really naive and stupid for trying to sleep with him. He was even more out of my league than I'd thought.

"It's just a house, Kai. It doesn't mean anything."

"Says people who live in houses like this." I paced the driveway. Oh God. I would look like I wanted Marcus for his money. I didn't. Again, I knew he had it, but being wealthy and having a house like this were two totally different things. What was I going to do? I'd thought I had an answer to my problems. I could try Ricky again, but I'd messaged him on Grindr to find out what happened the other night, and he hadn't responded. "Your neighbors are gonna call the cops on me if they see me around here."

"Then they'd have me to deal with. They know me and won't play that shit," Marcus replied, but I ignored him, wearing holes in my shoes from pacing. "Kai."

If I went back to Riverside, I could eventually save money and come back here, and even if it wasn't Santa Monica, I could move to LA. I could…

"*Kai.*" This time his voice was lower, more serious.

"What?" I stopped.

"This is four walls. It's not what's important in life. The structure doesn't matter, just the things that happen inside, and what happens in there is the same as what happens at that apartment we just left or where your folks live. It's where my family comes together."

He turned before I could respond and headed for the house. I was speechless for a moment. I'd never heard Marcus speak like that before, with such emotion and sincerity. And I knew without asking that when he said his family, he meant

Declan, Corbin, and Parker.

Marcus was sexy as fuck, but there was more to him than that, and for the first time in my life, I wanted to learn more about a man I was interested in. I wanted to figure him out, put his pieces together until I saw the whole of him.

"You gonna help me move shit in or what, baby?" I asked, using my best flirtatious voice.

"Yep. Just unlocking the door."

"What if I'd said no about staying?" I called out to him.

"Then I would have kidnapped you. I'm good at getting what I want."

I smiled at the laughter in his voice. I had no doubt he was right.

★ ★ ★

"FUCK. I HAVE a bathroom in my bedroom?" I said when we'd finished carrying everything inside.

"I think you might be the only person in the world to complain about that."

"Because I was hoping you'd accidentally walk in on me showering one day...or I'd come out in a towel and we'd run into each other in the hallway. My towel would fall, totally by accident, of course, and once you got an eye of me naked, no way you'd be able to resist." I pumped my brows playfully. Marcus shook his head, but I intrigued him. I could see that.

"Be good," he said again.

"Why do I have a feeling you're going to be telling me that a lot?"

"Because you're smart."

"Or because we both like it."

Marcus moaned, this deep growly sound that made my cock throb. "Stop tempting me."

"You're easily temptable," I countered. "Is that a word? If it's not, it is now." I enjoyed this back-and-forth between us. Marcus did too. If I didn't think so, I would have stopped doing it ages ago.

"Do you need my help in here?" he asked. "If not, I'm gonna get some things done."

"Scaredy-cat," I teased.

"I'm not scared. What would I be scared of?"

I felt entirely too proud of myself for getting to him this way because there was no doubt in my mind that's what was going on. "Me. You know, since you want me so much."

"I don't want you *that* much."

"Then why are you running from me?"

Amusement danced in Marcus's brown eyes. Did anyone work to get under his skin the way I did? For some reason, I didn't think so. Maybe the podcast guys, but that was in a different way from what I was doing.

"I'm not running from—why in the fuck do I argue with you? I know what you're doing."

I laughed. Fuck, he was fun. "I'm not doing anything other than letting you know when you're being sus."

"I'm not—goddamn it." He bit his cheeks in an obvious way to keep from smiling. "I can be around you. I'm not trying to escape you for any reason other than you're an annoying little shit and I'm actually going to research fish-tank moving companies *for* you."

Oh…well, damn. That was sweet. He came off so gruff sometimes, like he didn't care about anything, but I couldn't help wondering if there was a sweeter man in the world than Marcus Alston. Fine *and* caring? There had to be a mistake. He had to have some big-ass flaw I hadn't seen yet.

I stepped closer, didn't stop until I was looking up at him from inches away, the two of us breathing the same air.

"You're a teddy bear, Marcus."

"You're easily fooled."

I put a hand on his stomach, felt the tight muscles beneath his shirt, wished I could see him naked, all that beautiful brown skin on display for me to kiss and taste and savor. "Nope. I don't think so." I fisted my hand in his tee, making it rise some. The bulge behind the fly of his jeans was obvious. Damned if I wasn't hard too. I loved flirting, hooking up, having fun, but something about flirting with Marcus felt new and exciting. I'd never wanted anyone the way I wanted him. "You're sweet, and I think I'm gonna remind you of that as much as possible…until you believe it."

Marcus moved forward, backing me up until I hit the wall. He was breathing heavily, hot puffs against my face. He pressed his body against mine, hand moving up to my throat and holding it. Not tight, not restricting my airflow, but just there. He dropped his head forward, his mouth close to my ear, and goddamn it, he'd gotten the upper hand too fucking quickly. "Be careful, baby boy."

A wave of pleasure rolled down through my torso before landing in my groin. That was really fucking hot, and now I'd lost my train of thought. What had I even planned to say to him?

"Mmm…I felt that tremble. You want me, want this." He pumped his hips, making his cock rub against me.

"No shit," fell from my lips. I reached for him, but Marcus shook his head.

"Tsk, tsk. I didn't say you could touch." The motherfucker grinned because he knew he'd won. He let go of me and stepped away.

My whole body thrummed with want for him. "What! That's it?"

His smile turned into a deep, rumbly laugh. "I can tease

and play the game too, and I promise you, I always win. Now, can I go find a mover for you, or are you still trying to play in the big leagues?"

Oh, that's what I'd wanted to talk to him about. I fought to ignore the lust burning through me like wildfire. "I don't need you to fix everything for me. I'm a big boy. I can handle it myself."

"It's not a problem."

"I know. I can still do it myself." It was important to me to stand on my own two feet. Yeah, I had to live with him, but I didn't want to depend on him or anyone else. As much as I loved my family, that was part of why I left Riverside. I was the baby. They thought they had to protect me, and I didn't want that.

"Okay." He gave a curt nod, his gaze intense on me. Then without another word, he went for the door.

"I do appreciate it, Teddy."

He stopped, turned, and crossed his arms. "Teddy?"

"Yeah, I said you're a teddy bear, remember?"

"You're not calling me that."

"You don't know me at all, do you?"

He shook his head as if unsure what to do with me. He'd be doing that a lot. "I'm gonna change and go for a run. Figure out your mover situation, or I'll do it for you."

I decided to let that slide and, while he walked away, shouted, "Need to burn off all that pent-up energy from how much you want to fuck me?"

"You wish," he called back, but I knew I was right.

Chapter Seven

Marcus

I WORKED EVEN more than usual over the next few days. I also went for a lot of extra jogs and jerked off like I'd just found out what my dick could do. It was fucking torture living with Kai. He made me feel out of control, which was not something I was used to experiencing. He'd been right when he said I was avoiding him, that I wanted him too much, and the little shit made it obvious when we did happen to be at home together. The way he smirked, walked, stretched, bent over, fucking *breathed*. Everything he did got me hard.

It was annoying as hell.

"How's it going with Kai?" Corbin asked while we were getting changed at the gym to work out. We'd met here after work like we did sometimes. I grunted in reply, which did nothing except make my friend laugh. "That good, huh?"

"He's even more annoying than you."

"Hey—none of that. You want to fuck him, that's fine, but he doesn't get to annoy you more than me. That'll always be my job."

I smiled, tugged him close, and kissed his temple. "You'll always be my number one, kid."

"That's what I thought."

"That's not something to be happy about."

"It's part of my charm," he responded playfully.

We finished getting dressed and headed out of the locker room. Not only did I enjoy exercise, but I tried to go with Corbin as much as I could because he wouldn't overdo it with me there.

When we weren't talking, I was usually thinking about Kai. I was the kind of person who liked answers, who needed to understand the why of things. I liked things sorted into the correct boxes inside my head, but for whatever reason, I couldn't pin Kai down or why I wanted to so much. The power of my reaction to him didn't make sense, but if I could figure it out, then I'd know how to control it better.

Once we'd finished our workout, showered, and gotten dressed, I told Corb, "Let's go grab some dinner."

He nodded without arguing. There was a hibachi place within walking distance, so we headed there. When we were sitting with a plate of rice, chicken, and vegetables in front of us, Corb said, "Really, though, how's it going with Kai?"

"Fine. It's only been a few days. He's got a big-ass saltwater fish tank that's his baby. We got it delivered and set up yesterday. He fusses over them like they're his fucking kids. It's weird."

"God forbid someone have a pet they love."

"They're fish," I countered.

"Still living, breathing things, you jackass." Corbin laughed.

I popped a piece of grilled zucchini into my mouth. "He's close to his family. He talks to one of them on the phone every day."

"Wow, now that *is* weird. A family that's not dysfunctional?"

"Eh. I'm sure they are in their own way. Everyone is." My parents loved their work more than anything and were more like business partners than lovers. Corbin's parents loved the shit out of him but still believed he was going to hell for being queer. I didn't believe there was a family out there who wasn't fucked up in some ways. That's why I'd stick with Corbin, Parker, and Declan. "He does yoga in the living room," I added, surprising myself with how much I was talking about Kai.

"Damn. I love bendy men."

"You and me both, kid. Too bad I can't fuck him."

"Well, actually, you could. You're just a stubborn son of a bitch. You know what else you can do?"

Here we go. I should have known this was coming. "No, but I'm sure you'll enlighten me."

"Of course I will. It's why you love me." He leaned over the table as if he had to get close for what he had to say. "You could really get to know him if you wanted… You could date him. You're allowed to like him, in case you didn't know."

I groaned because it wasn't surprising he would say shit like that. I was lucky Parker wasn't here too. He'd definitely jump in on this. "I don't even know him. How could I like him?"

"Hence the whole getting-to-know-him thing."

So we could eventually end up miserable together? Living together but separate lives because we didn't like change? So we could let each other down time and time again? Fuck that. I was good without all that headache. "Eat your food."

"I am eating!" he countered. "And I don't know why you give me shit about it. I don't starve myself. I don't binge and purge. I watch my weight like the rest of us."

Corbin had been heavy as a kid. He hadn't quite grown into his looks yet at the time, some of his features more exaggerated than they were now. Coupled with being queer and how he'd been teased, it was the perfect storm to create his low self-esteem issues at a young age.

He'd done everything he could to change the exterior—weight loss, skin care, a little surgery, fillers, and just growing up and changing—but none of that had altered the pain inside. It was why he sought attention.

"You're beautiful, Corb."

"I know."

"You always have been."

He rolled his eyes without agreeing with that part. "Crushing on your roommate is making you mushier than usual."

"I'm not crushing on him." Fuck, had I ever crushed on anyone in my whole damn life? I wasn't sure I had.

"Yeah, okay. I suppose you don't have trust issues too? Oh, and you're not a workaholic!" He laughed, and damned if I didn't as well. There wasn't anyone I'd let get away with the shit Corbin, Declan, and Parker said to me, but then no one loved me the way they did either.

And I couldn't deny I let Kai get away with a whole lot too.

We chatted while we finished eating and then walked back to the lot where my car was. Corbin lived in a building not too far away, so he didn't drive here. We said our goodbyes and went our separate ways.

Kai's car was in the driveway when I got home, but I didn't see him in the living room. I went over to his tank, watched the fish swim around, the two clownfish staying together, one always following the other.

Somehow, I didn't hear him on the stairs, and then he was standing beside me. "Did you know all clownfish are born male? They can change due to their social environment. They pair up, and the dominant one becomes female. If the female dies, then the most dominant of the males left becomes biologically female and the alpha. It's crazy-interesting."

"No shit?" I turned to him, quirking a brow.

"Seriously. I wouldn't lie to you." He bumped my hip with his. He was wearing shorts, without a shirt. Corbin had been right—his nipples were pierced, a barbell through each. I wanted to tug on them with my teeth.

"You know a lot about fish."

"I was always interested in marine life."

"Is that something you want to do?"

"Do I have to want to do something other than be a bartender?"

Shit. I hadn't meant it like that, but I could see why he asked. He was always challenging me on things. "No."

"I know. But…I do…I think. I just haven't figured out what. Have you always wanted to be in real estate?" He sat down on my cream-colored couch and pulled his legs up under him. I found myself walking over and sitting on the opposite end.

"I have a degree in architecture. It's what my parents do. Alston Architecture." Kai shook his head as if to say he hadn't heard of it. "It's their baby. Neither of my parents came from shit. They worked really hard to succeed. When they did, they kept working, kept wanting more. It was never enough."

"They're still together?"

"Yeah, but I don't know if that's the right word for it. I assume they were passionate about each other at some point, but never in my lifetime. Sometimes I think they can't stand each other, or at least, they seem indifferent to each other. But they both love making money, and they're both good at it." Jesus, what was wrong with me? I couldn't believe I'd just said all that to him.

I was about to stand and go upstairs when Kai said, "Are they good to you?"

Shit. No one had ever asked me that. "They love me." And I knew they did. "I've never lacked for anything in my life. They opened a lot of doors for me, paved my way. The most sought-after architecture firm in California is Black-owned, and it'll be mine one day."

"That's not what I asked." He looked at me with that familiar challenge in his eyes, daring me to answer, telling me he would call me out if I didn't.

I didn't know how to back down. It wasn't how I was built. "Work always came first and always will. I've adjusted and understand."

He nodded, seemed to ponder that. "Is it enough for you?"

"Is what enough? My relationship with my parents? It doesn't matter how I feel. What matters is reality. I don't really do that—wish things could be different. Life is the way it is, and you adapt."

"I didn't mean that. I meant this." He made a sweeping motion, encompassing my house.

Oh. Because I'd said no matter how much they succeeded, it was never enough, so he was asking about my success. "Yes and no. I'll always strive to do better. It's important to me, but on the other hand, that's why I have Corbin, Declan, and Parker. They ground me, even if it does annoy the shit out of me."

"I don't believe that for a second. Okay, well, I guess I do believe it, but I think you keep them grounded even more." He nodded at me in another challenge, daring me to contradict him, telling me without words that he didn't think I would answer. And fuck if I didn't want to, even if only to prove him wrong. How in the fuck did he get me to react to him this way?

"We do that for each other," I said, then stood and moved

over in front of him. I wrapped a hand around his wrist and pulled Kai to his feet, our bodies touching the way they had in his room that first night. Leaning down, I ran my nose along his cheek, then down to his neck. Kai trembled beneath my touch. "You're always trying to get under my skin." This time, I brushed my lips over his heated skin, peppering kisses along the way.

"I'm good at getting to you," Kai replied, breathless.

"Yes." I kissed his throat. "You." I pressed my lips along his jaw. "Are." The word was spoken hovering over his mouth, just touching enough that we could feel each other, a tease of what I considered giving him, before pulling away.

"Motherfucker," Kai groaned when I took a step back. "You're going to kill me."

"I always win, baby boy. You might have gotten secrets out of me, but I still ended the night on top."

"You can end the night on top of me if you'd like."

My chuckle was impossible to hold back. "I'm good."

"Your dick is going to pop out of your pants. All you did was turn yourself on, and now you're gonna have to go to your room and…oh God. You're gonna be jacking off in your room."

A full-fledged laugh escaped me. He was something else. "Good night, Kai."

"I'll leave my door open if you change your mind," he called after me as I went for the stairs. "Where I'll be jerking my dick and thinking about you."

"How many times have I told you you're playing with fire?"

"I know, I know. I guess you don't realize how much I really want to be burned."

Damned if I didn't want him just as much. Still, I went to my room, grabbed my laptop, and worked for hours. When I finally climbed into bed, Kai was in my thoughts as I came all over my chest.

And I knew it was only a matter of time before he got exactly what we both wanted.

Chapter Eight

Kai

"HOW ARE THINGS going living with Marcus?" Declan asked at work on Saturday evening. One look told me it had been killing him not to ask me all week. There wasn't a doubt in my mind he'd talked to Marcus about it, but I didn't figure Marcus gave him much info.

"Really good. He gives the best head I've ever had. This one time, he did this thing with his fingers…" I trembled dramatically. "Well, let's just say a gentleman never tells."

Declan crossed his arms, leaning against the counter. "You're a brat."

"Gasp! You don't believe me?"

He chuckled. "You're not sleeping with Marcus."

"No, but can you put in a good word for me?" That earned me another chuckle before I got serious. "It's great. I live in a big, beautiful home with a fine-ass man who's equal parts kind and infuriating. And he loves my fish. I catch him watching them often. It's adorable. He's done all this research on them and asks me questions. He literally bought a new filter because he wasn't sure the one I had was good enough and thought it might cause problems—spoiler: mine was good, but it was sweet anyway. Most of the time I don't let him do stuff for me, but I let that one slide." I began wiping down the counters. Luckily, we weren't too busy yet.

"Yep. That sounds like Marcus. Biggest heart out of any of us but doesn't see it."

"Or maybe he just doesn't want attention for it. Maybe he does the things he does because it's important to him and not to be praised for it." I didn't know why I thought that or why I was telling Declan something about the man he'd been best friends with since he was a kid. He was right, I figured. Marcus didn't see it, but if he ever did, I didn't think he'd like it being brought up. "Sorry. Not that I think I know him better than you. I don't really know him at all."

That didn't feel right, though. I could see the person Marcus was, and I felt a strange connection to that.

"No worries. You're right. He's never wanted a big deal being made about the things he does."

"Can I ask how you met?"

Declan glanced over his shoulder and said, "Just a sec," before going to help a customer and then coming back to me. "Marcus and Corbin met online. It was a message board for queer people. Neither was out yet, so they bonded over that but had never met. Me and Park had become friends—well, he pushed his friendship on me."

"And it was the best thing to ever happen to you."

"That and Sebastian, yeah. But anyway, so they were talking, and me and Parker were talking. Corbin had some struggles in school, and after an embarrassing incident, Park went to comfort him. I always went where Parker did, so then the two of us got close to Corb, and we all met up with Marcus."

"He didn't go to the same school?"

"Nope. He went to private school."

For whatever reason, it made me sad to think about him being away from them. Had Marcus had anyone at his school he could be himself around? Be close with? As much as he said his parents loved him, they hadn't been close, so all I could picture was Marcus being alone. An ache started deep in my chest, a constant throb there.

"We used to ride the bus to his house. His parents were always working, so it was our hangout. I stayed with him sometimes when shit was going down in my life. Half the time, his mom and dad didn't even know."

"Yeah, he told me they're workaholics and didn't have much time for him."

Wrinkles formed on Declan's forehead as his brows drew together. "He told you that?"

My pulse skittered beneath my skin. "Yeah, is that a big deal?" The question was dumb and maybe kinda fishing because I knew the answer. I'd known it as Marcus was talking to me the other night. He didn't offer pieces of himself to just anyone, and he didn't do it freely. I wasn't sure what it meant that he'd shared with me, but I recognized the gift he'd given me.

"It's...interesting," Dec replied. "I just—"

"Nope. Sorry, handsome. You're not doing that. People joke around and call Marcus Daddy—*hot*, by the way—but I'm thinking that's also you. There's nothing you need to worry about."

"Fine, you're right. I don't understand this. My whole life, I had Marcus, Parker, and Corbin and no one else. Then I fell in love with Bastian, and now I'm *feeling* things all the time. I have more friends, and I'm always worrying about others. It's annoying."

"Do you know you? You've always been a caretaker, Declan. You and Marcus have that in common. Now, leave me alone so I can work. My boss is a real asshole."

"Sometimes I think you forget you're talking to your boss when you are."

"I don't forget anything, handsome." I winked and walked away.

A few minutes later my cell vibrated against my leg. We weren't busy, so I tugged it out, surprised to see Archer's name on the screen. He was one of the few people I used to feel fairly close to. We'd hung out often for a few years before he moved to Atlanta.

"Can I take my break?" I asked Declan, who said yes.

"Hey...you're calling. People never call nowadays," I joked as I made my way through the back door and outside.

Archer laughed. "This is important, so I figured it required more than a text. Are you still bartending at Driftwood?"

"Yep." Why was he asking me that?

"I have a proposition for you. I'm working on opening a new bar in Midtown. I'm going to need good people to work with me, and someone who can be my right-hand man. Someone like you. You're good at socializing and publicity, and we both know I can be a bit of a dick." Archer chuckled.

Was he asking me what I thought he was?

"Anyway, it's gonna be lit. I have a great building. It was a gay bar that closed down, and we're remodeling it." Archer was a trust-fund baby and had the money for something like this. I imagined whatever he was doing would succeed. "I have a shitload of plans. I'll email you photos and what I'm thinking. Can you imagine what we could do together?"

Archer had always been fun. He wasn't lying that he could be a jerk, but not always. People wanted to spend time with him, and yeah, a club run by him? The possibilities were endless.

My heart raced, but my stomach twisted, unsure. "Are you asking me if I want to run a gay bar with you? Just making sure I'm understanding you right."

He gave another chuckle. "Yeah, man. What do you think? We can discuss wages and all, but you know I'll do you right."

"Why me?"

"Because I need someone I can trust."

That made sense, but I was still trying to wrap my head around the fact that he was opening a bar and wanted me to move to Atlanta to work with him.

"Shit's pretty fly out here. There's a good gay scene. It's not nearly as expensive as LA. You should see the apartments you can get for less than what you'd find in Los Angeles for double the price."

"I…" Didn't know what to say. Part of me wanted to jump at the opportunity, but then I thought of my family. Mom thought I was too far away already. On the other hand, I was trying to figure out who I was. Hell, I couldn't even afford my own place in Santa Monica. "Yes," fell from my lips before I could think about it too much.

"Fuck yes! I knew you'd be down."

Archer gave me a little more information on what he planned and what I would be doing. It was a whirlwind of him yammering in my ear while I tried to make sense of what just happened. Before I knew it, he was telling me to expect an email with the details, then ended the call.

I was going to be someone's right-hand man to run a new gay bar.

I was moving to Atlanta.

I'd have to tell my mom…

And then, for whatever the fuck crazy reason, I thought of Marcus, of spending time with him and the things he'd shared with me. How I wanted to get to know him even more, and yet I also knew he only let me stay with him out of some misguided hero complex. It would probably be a relief for him to know he wouldn't have to share his house with me for long.

★ ★ ★

"SO...IS THIS WHAT we husbands do every week while our men are recording their podcast?" I teased Sebastian and Elliott, who were sitting in the living room. I'd just woken up a little while before and came downstairs to find Marcus gone and these two here. I'd forgotten they recorded every Sunday, and this would be my first one here for it.

I'd listened to a few episodes of *The Vers*, but I wasn't a regular. It was popular as fuck, though, and I'd always thought it was cool that my boss was a part of it. But I'd also planned on talking to Marcus about Atlanta today, and this threw a wrench into my plans. Strangely, I wanted to talk to him about it before I told Declan, which made no sense, considering Declan was my boss and I'd known him longer.

Elliott chuckled. "Yep. They'll be in there for a while."

"We usually hang out for a bit afterward," Sebastian added.

"This is the spot, huh?" I asked, not at all surprised. Declan had mentioned they used to spend a lot of time in Marcus's childhood home, and every time they spoke about hanging out now, it was almost always here.

"It is," Sebastian said. "Oh God. I remember the first time I came here. I was scared to death. I was falling for Declan and worried they wouldn't like me. I knew how much they meant to him." Sebastian ran a hand through his dark, wavy hair.

"Well, at least you didn't drunk-marry their romantic in Vegas the night you told him you couldn't see yourself ever really falling for someone and wanting forever," Elliott chimed in.

"Good point," Sebastian agreed.

"I worried Marcus or Declan would kill me, and they'd never find the body."

"They almost did."

Watching Elliott and Sebastian go back and forth, I felt a stab of…hell, I couldn't place it. Longing? I didn't have a lot of friends. I had acquaintances. I could always find someone to fuck or party with, someone to go out dancing with if I wanted, but not real friends like *The Vers* guys and now their partners. People didn't tend to stick around a lot with me.

And then I thought about Archer and Atlanta. Maybe I could find there what *The Vers* guys had. Maybe that would have been me and Archer if he hadn't moved.

I smiled when I saw my hazelnut creamer sitting by the coffeepot. Marcus didn't use it, so unless one of the guys did, he'd taken it out for me. That didn't make me special to Marcus. I understood it was just the kind of man he was, but it still felt good.

I doctored my cup while they chatted, then made my way over to the couch. I heard laughter from the studio, Marcus's deeper than the rest. They had fun together, and I liked hearing or seeing him have fun. I also wanted to have naked fun with him, so yeah, that was still a thing.

And now there was a timeframe in place for that.

I said, "You know how sports spouses all have some kind of nickname? I think you guys should too. What would you be…the poddies?"

That made Elliott and Sebastian laugh.

"Sounds like someone has to use the bathroom. They also call themselves the Beach Bums. Maybe something with that," Elliott said. It was cool how neither of them was ever jealous. You could tell they knew how special the friendship was between the four men, but that it didn't change how much Declan or Parker loved them.

"Okay, explain this Beach Bums thing to me." I took a sip of my coffee, then set it on the side table.

"When they were kids, they'd go to the beach to look at men's asses, and called themselves the Beach Bums so no one would know," Sebastian answered.

"Bum—ass. I see where this is going."

"That's also where the name of Parker's bakery—Beach Buns—came from."

"Well, shit. Aren't they the cutest things?" I said, earning another chuckle.

They kept me in the loop while they talked—about the guys, but also about Elliott's work as a city planner, and the screenplays Sebastian was writing and what his plans were for the future. Every once in a while, I'd hear laughter or arguing coming from the studio.

I finished my coffee, stood, and stretched just as the door opened. Marcus came out first, and his hot stare immediately went to me, starting at my head, then traveling down my body before going up again. I swear I fucking *felt* the way he looked at me, the desire skating across my skin. I glanced down at myself. I was wearing small cotton shorts and a cropped T-shirt.

"'Morning, Teddy," I said.

"It's afternoon," he countered, and then his eyes widened as he realized what I'd called him. "Oh fuck."

"Teddy?" Corbin asked. "*Teddy?* What the fuck is that nickname for, and please explain the story behind it."

Oops.

"Don't do it," Marcus warned.

"Do what? Tell them I call you Teddy because—oh my God!" I ran when Marcus came after me. He wrapped one arm around my waist, and the other hand went over my mouth.

He lifted me up, saying, "Be good," while he tried to tug

me out of the room.

I fought him, working to break free. When I licked his hand, he pulled it back, and I said, "You can't talk to me like that unless we're having sex." His hand went to my mouth again. I wiggled until I fell out of his arms, my ass hitting the ground. I looked up at him. "I expect you to kiss it and make it better."

He rolled his eyes before grabbing my hand and drawing me to my feet.

"You should check for bruises." I looked over my shoulder and down at my butt.

"You're fine."

"Thank you." I smiled.

"That's not what I meant."

I frowned. "So I'm not hot?"

He shook his head just as Corbin's voice broke through this little game we were playing. "Anyone else feel like they walked into an alternate universe? It's like I don't even know Marcus anymore."

Marcus's attention snapped to his friends as if he'd forgotten we weren't alone.

"Yep, I do," Parker responded.

"Count me in," Declan added.

"Here too." Elliott raised a hand.

"I think it's sweet." Sebastian grinned.

"*Sweet?*" Marcus said. "He makes me crazy."

"Hey. That wasn't nice." I pouted.

"Are you kidding? It's your goal."

Okay, maybe he was right. "Yeah, well, it's different for me to want that than for you to say it," I teased.

"I don't understand you." Marcus walked toward the kitchen. "Don't say a word," he told Corbin, Declan, and Parker.

Everyone other than Marcus laughed.

Chapter Nine
Marcus

IT WOULD BE a cold day in hell before I would admit this to anyone, but I agreed with Corbin—it almost felt like I was living in an alternate universe. Whatever the fuck that was I'd done with Kai was so out of the ordinary for me that I was starting to wonder if someone had slipped me something. Was I high? I didn't feel high, but I also didn't wrestle with men I wanted to fuck either, so who knew?

I tried not to grumble as I pulled the seasoned chicken out of the fridge for the grill.

"You good?" Parker asked me quietly.

"Why wouldn't I be?" I replied as if I didn't know why he'd asked. "You bring dessert?" Parker was a baker. I'd helped him acquire the building, and the business was thriving.

"Of course. And I brought a pineapple upside-down cake just for you."

"Good man." I loved that shit. I wasn't big on desserts, but that was my favorite.

"I'll help you." Parker and I carried the food outside, where I had the grill and a full kitchen. Kai was talking to Elliott and Corbin when we passed by, and he winked at me before kissing the air. I almost smiled but stopped myself. All it would do was encourage him. I needed to chill the fuck out where Kai was concerned.

Everyone came outside. The kitchen was to the right, chairs and tables in the center, and a pool in front of us. If you walked along the path by the pool, it led to the beach, and on the other side of a white, veil-style fence, I had a firepit with built-in chairs in the sand. It was a lot, I got that, but I liked having a place where all of us could be, liked knowing that if Corbin, Parker, or Declan ever needed somewhere to stay, they had a place here. The four of us—well, shit, the six of us now—had everything we could possibly need right at our fingertips. We'd consoled Parker after bad dates here, we'd supported Declan because of his asshole father here, and we'd done our best to make Corbin feel beautiful here as well.

"Hey, baby. You're spacing out." Kai leaned against the house, watching me stand in front of the open grill.

"Is it baby or Teddy?"

He shrugged. "I don't know. It depends on my mood. Which do you like better?"

"Marcus," I replied.

"Liar."

I finished putting the food on, set the utensils down, and closed the lid. "You're trouble."

"Nah, not trouble. I just challenge you. No one else does that." He didn't try to hide the fact that he was admiring me, his warm stare taking me in. "Go swimming with me."

"No."

"Fine. Maybe Corbin wants to go." He moved to walk away, but my arm shot out, hand against the house, blocking him in.

"No," I said again.

"No? This isn't one of the times you get to tell me what to do."

"No, you can't make me jealous with my best friend."

"So you admit you would be?" He licked his lips.

My skin heated, a bead of perspiration running down the side of my neck. "Not what I was saying. It's not possible with them. I might play around like it is, but it's not." Because even if I never let myself have Kai, they knew I wanted him and would never do that to me.

"Ah, gotchu. You already staked a claim. If that's the case...when are you going to take what's yours?" Kai asked, surprising me by stepping close and licking that bead of sweat from my skin. "I'll tell you a secret... I flirt with them for fun. You're the one I want."

My stomach flipped in a way I was unfamiliar with. Before I could respond or try to get the upper hand, Kai sneaked under my arm, tugging his shirt off while he walked, then jumped into the pool.

"Let's go swimming," Corbin said, not surprisingly. He turned to me. "Come on, Marcus. I'll get in and out to watch the food."

I motioned for him to go ahead. He cocked his brow in a silent question: *you sure?* When I nodded, he stripped down to his underwear and jumped in. Elliott and Parker were next, followed by Sebastian taking his clothes off. He tried to remove Dec's too, but my friend shook his head, pushed his boyfriend into the water, then made his way over to me.

We watched them together, Parker and Elliott trying to dunk Sebastian, and Corbin lifting Kai to his shoulders before the two of them crashed into the water again. "They're all like a bunch of fucking kids," I said, noticing the amusement in my own voice.

"Yeah, but it's kinda great, isn't it? I love that we have this. I never thought I'd have anything until I had you, Park, and Corb, and now we have them too."

"Damn, boy. Falling in love has put you in touch with your feelings," I teased, earning a chuckle.

"It's annoying as shit. I try not to do it often. I just like seeing Sebastian this way. Having fun with friends, with people who don't give a shit if he ever acts in another movie or not."

"I hear ya."

I had a feeling something was coming in three…two…one… "You're different with Kai."

"He's a pain in my ass."

Declan chuckled. "Yeah, I know. He's a pain in mine too sometimes. But he's a good guy. There's something about him. I took to him too—in a different way than you, of course."

I didn't look at Declan, keeping my features schooled, watching Kai enjoy himself with my family. He ducked his head under the water, trying to escape Parker. When he burst through the surface again, he had the biggest smile on his face, which I fucking *felt* just looking at him. It was like people around him fed off his happiness and zest for life and… What. The. Fuck. Was I even thinking?

"Maybe I should just fuck him and get it over with," I mused. I could get this craving for him out of my system. There was no fear of it being awkward afterward. Kai didn't want more from me other than my dick. He was young, and I'd just be that guy he'd had an orgasm with as he figured out what he wanted in life.

Declan said, "I can't believe this is happening."

"You sounded supportive two seconds ago," I countered.

"Yeah, well, I was worried at first, but now I'm not because I think you actually have a little crush on someone for the first time in your life. I'm here to tell you, even when it feels like torture, it's not. So I *am* supportive. Just shocked."

The hairs on my arms stood on end. "I don't like him. You sound like Parker now. Is this what happens when people fall in love?"

"Maybe you'll be able to answer that question next."

"Bite your tongue." I grabbed Declan, wrestling him toward the pool. I meant to push him in, but the crafty little fucker grabbed me, and the two of us fell in together, fully clothed.

"I did it!" Declan cheered.

"I'll have my revenge," I replied, making my way to the stairs to get out. Before I could, arms wrapped around my shoulders, and legs entangled themselves around my waist.

"Now that you're here, I'm not letting you escape," Kai said.

"I have to cook."

"I can finish up," Elliott said.

"There's not one person here I trust with my grill."

"I'm Cuban. I understand seasonings," Elliott teased, making me laugh.

Still, I patted Kai's thigh. "Let go. I'm gonna finish what I was doing."

I was surprised when he did it easily, but as I climbed out of the water, he said, "I'm determined to make you start having fun. I hope you know when I want something, I don't give up until I make it happen."

Yeah, there wasn't a part of me that didn't believe him.

"Wait…are you saying we're not fun?" Corbin asked. "I make Marcus have a good time quite often."

"Maybe you can give me pointers," Kai told him.

"You two aren't allowed to hang out," I joked, tugging off my shirt and laying it over the back of a chair to dry. Luckily, I was wearing shorts, so those weren't as bad as if I'd been wearing jeans.

"I got your back," Corbin told him.

Great. There was no doubt in my mind I was now fucked.

They continued to enjoy themselves while Elliott helped me cook. They got out when it was time to eat, the seven of us sitting around the table outside. It was loud the way it always was when my friends were here, but Kai made the tempo even more upbeat. The guy felt like he had endless energy, which again, was something else people fed off around him.

"Okay, someone tell me stories about Marcus. I need more dirt," Kai said when we finished eating but were still sitting together.

"Time for everyone to leave," I told them. When no one moved, I added, "I'm not playin'."

"I love Beach Bums stories," Sebastian said. He was probably one of the most earnest people I'd ever met, and while in many ways he felt like the complete opposite of Declan, they worked together.

"I have one," Elliott said, making me frown. "This one time, he wanted to kick my ass because he thought I was going to break Parker's heart."

"In my defense, it was Corbin who said he'd hire a hitman."

"How is that a defense?" Elliott countered. He turned to Corb. "I thought we were cool."

"We are. *Now.* We had to make sure you were worthy of our boy. You are."

Parker said, "Actually, it was Marcus who defended us the most then. He told me to trust myself and gave me a wake-up call in a way only Marcus can—with brutal honesty."

I pointed to him and Elliott. "Looks like it worked out. You're welcome. Now, let's tell Corbin stories. There are more to choose from, and they're more ridiculous than the rest of ours." I was at the head of the table, with Corbin on one side and Kai on the other.

Corb playfully kicked my shin. "Ignore him."

They, in fact, ignored my ass, telling Kai about dumb shit we'd done as kids or things that made Kai say *aww*. The funny, quirky stories were mixed in with ones about me being the voice of reason in the group, which were my favorite. I couldn't pretend it wasn't interesting to see myself through their eyes, though. It always made me feel different, better.

When Parker talked about how I'd taken him to his high school prom, complete with dinner and flowers as if it were a real date, Kai said, "I rest my case on why I call him a teddy bear."

I rolled my eyes, but my chest was tight. Everyone talking about me was making me uncomfortable. "Well, that's about enough of that shit." I pushed to my feet and grabbed my plate.

There was more laughter, but everyone followed me, cleaning up the mess and bringing the dishes inside.

"We'll help you get everything cleaned up before we head out," Parker said.

"I got it. You guys can go. After I finish in the kitchen, I've got to update some listings. My work phone has been going off all day."

"It's Sunday," Kai said.

"We should help first," Corb said, but it was Kai who waved them off.

"Marcus cooked, so I'll clean up. It's what good little houseboys do."

"You've never been good a day in your life," I teased.

"Ask nicely, and I'll be real good for you."

That one sentence, coupled with the way he looked at me, made blood rush to my groin. I tried to pretend his words didn't get to me, but I was sure everyone knew they did. "Be quiet before I send you to your room." I turned to the guys. "Now get out. I have shit to do," I said playfully, but that lit a fire under them, and we all said our goodbyes.

This was usually when I noticed how quiet the house felt without them, but then Kai said, "No work on Sundays."

"Not your call, baby boy."

I went to the sink and turned on the water to start the dishes.

Chapter Ten

Kai

"HAS ANYONE EVER told you you're the most stubborn man in the world?" I went to the sink and nudged him with my hip. "Move over. I'll wash. You put them in the dishwasher." Because Marcus was one of those people who cleaned their dishes before loading them to be washed a second time. I'd argued with him about it enough, so I let that go.

He scooted his muscular body to the left. "You know most people don't tell me what to do, right?"

"You realize I'm not most people, *right*?" I tossed back. He grumbled under his breath, but when I washed a plate and gave it to him, he put it in the dishwasher. "I think your nickname should have been The Workaholic instead of The Realist." When he didn't respond, I said, "The Grump?" Then I deepened my voice, "The Intimidator... You could have your own superhero movie!"

A smile tugged at the corners of his mouth. Marcus visibly tried to fight it, but then surprised me by saying, "I'll be back," in an Arnold Schwarzenegger voice.

"Oh my God! The Stubborn made a joke."

"I make jokes all the time, and The Stubborn doesn't make sense."

"It does if people know you," I countered, enjoying this.

Marcus was more than just a sexy man. He fascinated me. Not that I didn't want to bone him, because obviously, I did, but I also wanted to learn all the things I could about him. I wanted to find every way I could to make him laugh and smile...and come. I wanted to do nice things for him because he did them for everyone around him every day, and I worried he thought that was where his worth lay.

"What about you?" he asked, which I hadn't expected at all. "If you were a member of *The Vers*, who would you be?"

"You tell me, Teddy."

"The Brat." He cocked a brow.

"I can work with that. What else?"

"The Flirt, The Frustrating, The Infuriating."

"Hey! That's basically the same as The Frustrating...and maybe I'll slow down when you stop pretending you don't like it."

We spent the next little while naming each other and laughing while we washed the dishes together. It was totally different from anything I'd ever done with a man I wanted to fuck before, but I wasn't complaining. I liked Marcus's company too much for that.

But then all I could think about was the fact that I was moving, and it felt strangely gross that I hadn't told Marcus, even though it had just happened. "So...I have good news for you."

"What is it?"

"I should be out of your hair soon. I don't have an exact date. Archer is supposed to let me know, but he said in the next couple of months."

Marcus turned to me. "Who the fuck is Archer?"

Shit. I guess I should explain. "He's an old friend, someone I used to hang out with. He moved to Atlanta a couple of years ago. He's opening his own queer bar, and he asked me to help run it with him. As soon as he lets me know it's time, I'll be going there. Atlanta's not as expensive as it is here, so that will help. I haven't told Declan yet, or my mom, but…" But I was rambling, for some weird-ass reason. "So that's it. I'm going to move to Atlanta and help run a bar."

"Is that a smart decision? These kinds of things often don't go as planned, and then you're going to be halfway across the country without family or a safety net."

"Marcus…"

"Do you have a contract? I can look it over for you."

"There is no contract, but he sent me a ton of other info—my wages and about the bar."

"Kai, you can't just drop everything and move because of something some guy you used to know said. You have to protect yourself. You—"

"Marcus," I said again, closing my eyes. "Please don't ruin this for me. I'm excited. This feels like an answer to my recent problems. Archer is my friend. I can trust him. Plus, I'll be careful. We'll figure out a contract or agreement. Just…be happy for me. This is a really good opportunity for me. And for you. I won't be annoying you anymore." I nudged him again.

"It's not in my DNA not to worry about these things."

"I'm not your responsibility."

He hesitated for a moment, then said, "No, I guess you're not. Keep me posted."

And I knew that was that, at least for tonight.

When we finished the dishes, he grabbed a towel and gave it to me. "My hero," I teased, trying to lighten the mood. I dried my hands before giving it back to him. Even in that, he was a gentleman. He'd passed it to me before using it himself. If I were the swooning sort, Marcus would make me do it often.

I leaned against the counter, with Marcus standing right in front of me, so close I could feel the heat radiating off his beautiful skin.

"You don't go out much," he said unexpectedly.

"How do you know? I've only been living here for a week." Marcus shrugged, not explaining himself. But the truth was, he was right. "I work a lot, and mostly use an app when I want to fuck someone. I have to admit I usually would have done that already, but the only person I want to fuck right now is standing in front of me."

If my words got to him, Marcus didn't show it. Whatever he was feeling at the moment, he was trying to hide and succeeding.

"Did you fuck Archer?"

"Jealous?" I countered.

He shrugged.

"No."

"Friends?" He raised his hand and cupped my cheek, brushing his thumb over my skin.

"There are people I chill with, but nothing like you have, if that's what you're asking. I'm…a lot for most people, but I'm damn sure not going to change who I am for others. I like me." At some point, he'd moved even closer, pressing his hard, thick cock against me and making lust coil deep in my gut. "You got me a gift," I said, pushing into him so he knew I meant his dick. "I want it. Are you going to let me have it, or are we going to keep dancing around how much we want each other? Who knows how much time we'll have." Which was true. At least a couple of months, but that wasn't forever.

"You're the most frustrating guy I've ever met."

"Because you want me more than anyone else?"

"It'll just be sex. That's all I have to offer."

"Keepin' it real like always, huh? But who said I wanted

more? Or that I have more to offer you? I want to have sex with you, Marcus. I'm not asking you to be my boyfriend. Hell, I'm not even asking you for monogamy. Just your dick. Could be a fun way to spend our time until I move."

Before I had the chance to wrap my head around what was happening, Marcus's mouth slammed down on mine. He kissed the way he did everything—completely in control—skilled and measured like he was a world-renowned expert. I wasn't embarrassed of how I whimpered when his tongue took possession of my mouth, his hard body the most delicious pressure against mine.

I shoved my hand between us, rubbed his thick cock that I couldn't wait to play with. Marcus held me with one hand on either side of my face while his tongue took what it wanted from my mouth.

"Where are you going?" I asked when he pulled back, but his eyes were filled with the same hungry desire I felt for him.

Marcus grabbed the bottom of my shirt, so I lifted my arms and let him take it off. He bent forward, lashing his tongue over one of my pierced nipples before using his teeth to gently tug on the barbell there.

"Fuuuuck." I clutched the back of his head, his short hair prickly against my palm as I held him there, pushed him closer so he could keep tormenting my nipple with his mouth. My cock throbbed. I was pretty sure all the blood in my whole body had collected there and I was going to die from the world's hardest erection.

I continued to rub his dick with my right hand, wishing he were naked so I could taste him. When my left loosened on his head, Marcus pulled back. "Go to my room."

"Now *this* is one of those times you're allowed to be bossy to me."

"Finally, a time when you'll listen," he teased.

"Oh, I'll still only obey when I want to. But that's part of the fun, right?"

He smiled, maybe the biggest smile I'd ever seen from Marcus, and damned if it didn't make him even sexier. "You're a handful."

"So are you." I palmed his dick again but then said, "Race you to your room," and took off for the stairs.

Marcus didn't run, though. I turned and watched him slowly stalk after me. I didn't figure Marcus rushed for anyone. He did everything at his own pace.

As soon as I got to his room, I pulled off my shorts and underwear as I took in the space. His whole house was bougie as shit, but his bedroom was like his fucking palace.

He had a huge bed with a large, white, cloth-covered headboard. It looked like a bed for a king, which was what he deserved. The rest of the room had the typical stuff, including a bathroom off it, but the most amazing feature was directly in front of his bed—two accordion glass doors that opened onto a large balcony, where I could see a hot tub and a futon stacked with pillows, all with the view of the golden coast as a backdrop.

What the fuck was I doing here? I felt like Julia Roberts in *Pretty Woman*, only ya know, he wasn't paying me to be with him.

"I like boys who are prepared." Marcus palmed the cheeks of my ass, spreading them.

"Speaking of being prepared, unless I excuse myself for a bit, I'm not sure this is the best time for butt stuff. Sorry. I should have mentioned that before." He was quiet. Shit. Now I'd disappointed him. "I can go take care of it, but only because—"

"No." He wrapped his arms around me from behind, then fisted my cock, slowly stroking me. "There are other things we can do. I want you too much to wait."

"That makes two of us." I leaned back against him while Marcus lazily jacked me off. He was still dressed, his clothes rough against my skin, while one of his hands moved over to play with my full balls.

"Pretty cock on a pretty boy."

My knees went weak. If he hadn't been holding me up, I was pretty sure I would have collapsed. "Don't make me come yet. I wanna suck you off, want to make you bust a nut before you do the same for me."

Marcus fucking growled, nuzzling his face into my neck. "Christ, you're going to be the death of me." He pulled back. "Open the doors."

"So bossy."

"Stop pretending you don't like it."

I walked over and pushed open one, then the other. The sound of the ocean filled the room, the sun slowly slipping lower in the sky.

When I turned around, Marcus was naked, and goddamn. If I thought he was sexy before, there was nothing like seeing him bare. His abs looked like they'd been sculpted out of stone, his nipples dark against his skin that was a shade or two a lighter brown.

I loved the tattoo in the middle of his chest, a skull with roses on each side.

I didn't move from the doorway, waiting until Marcus walked over to me. "Fuck, you're so damn fine, Marcus."

"You too. I can't wait to see you on your knees."

Oh, well, hello there. I trembled. That had been really fucking hot. I knelt, not needing him to tell me twice. Marcus held the base of his cock—thick and beautiful and mouthwatering. I tilted my head up, and he traced my lips with the tip. When he eased back, I licked them. I could taste his precum there.

Marcus kept his dark pubes short and neatly trimmed. He took a step, pushing up on his toes so his nuts met my mouth. I smiled before dipping lower so he could flatten his feet while I lavished his balls. They tasted like salt and smelled so fucking good, a heady mixture of musk and fading soap. His sac was tight. I kissed it, licked it, nuzzled into him, inhaling his scent, letting his short, coarse hairs prickle my tongue.

"I love cock," I said.

"Lick it."

"My pleasure." I did as he said, starting at his balls and letting my tongue make the long journey up his shaft until I hit the tip.

"Open," Marcus said, and I did that too, looking up at him as he pushed his cock past my lips, stretching them. He fucked into me gently and slowly, in short thrusts like he was letting me get used to him. My dick and balls were throbbing with the need for release, but I wanted to work a load out of Marcus before I let myself come.

When he stopped moving, he didn't need words to tell me it was my turn to do the work. I wrapped a hand around him, sucking him while I bobbed my head, savoring the heat that radiated off him.

Marcus's hand, which was bigger than mine, held my head, thumb brushing against my scalp as he said, "Fuck, that's it. I knew you'd have a good mouth. Gonna keep you down there, sucking my cock every time I want to shoot my load."

My dick twitched, his words fueling me, making me take him deeper, wanting this to be the best blowjob Marcus had ever had, wanting him to lose control, fuck my mouth, and then come down my throat.

"Christ," he said, pulling back, panting, then rubbing his

spit-slicked cock and balls all over my face.

I fucking loved it.

"You're already going to make me blow my load."

I winked up at him. "I'm good at this. Let me lie on the bed with my head hanging over. You can fuck my throat like that. It's my favorite."

He moaned before pulling me to my feet and lifting me. My arms and legs immediately wrapped around him as his mouth crushed mine again. He kissed me, one arm around me, the other on my ass, kneading my cheek. He walked to the bed and lay down on top of me, thrusting and slowly making out with me. Or dicks rubbed together, the most delicious friction that threatened to make me lose control. "Stop if you don't want me to come now."

"I thought younger men were supposed to last longer?" He smirked.

"Fuck you." I laughed, enjoying this Marcus.

He moved off me, and I positioned myself with my head hanging off the side of the bed. He spread his legs, standing over me so I could love on his sac again, sucking his heavy balls into my mouth. At the same time, he spit in his hand, then stroked my cock, which I knew had to be leaking all over the damn place. When the muscles in my stomach tightened, he let go, knowing I was close to losing it.

"Show me what else this sexy mouth of yours can do. You have to earn the load in my balls if you want it."

"Fuck...I want it so much." I was dying for it, starving for his cum.

Marcus pushed into my mouth, starting easy before picking up the pace and fucking into me. My lips stretched, my eyes watered, my throat burned, but when he tried to ease off, I wrapped a hand around the back of his thigh, holding him in place and letting him know I wanted it.

He went at me more, harder, but always careful. It was never too much, and I knew if it were, Marcus would sense it and stop. My body felt like electric currents were shooting beneath my skin, like I could come without a hand on me, just by letting Marcus fuck my throat.

When his movements turned jerkier, his breathing faster, I knew I was about to earn my reward for a job well done.

"Fuck…I'm gonna come, baby boy. Gonna shoot my load in your mouth, and I want you to swallow it all up."

As soon as I nodded, his dick pulsed in my mouth, the hot spray of his salty release filling it. I swallowed and kept letting him use my mouth until his balls were wrung dry and my stomach was sated with what he'd given me.

My whole body melted into the bed. I couldn't move, but it turned out I didn't have to. Marcus leaned over me and sucked my cock deep into his mouth, bobbing on me while using his hand to stroke me at the same time.

The currents in my skin exploded, sunbursts of pleasure igniting inside me as pulse after pulse of my load spurted into his mouth, Marcus taking it all down the way I had with him.

He rolled off me after, lying in the opposite direction, both of us breathing heavily.

When I got myself under control, I said, "Told you you were missing out. Why did you make us wait so long to do that?"

"So fucking mouthy," he replied, but I knew without looking he had a smile on his face.

I leaned over, kissed his soft cock, then straddled him as my lips trailed up his torso until I got to his mouth. My tongue slipped inside, tasting myself on him, before I climbed off and said, "Thanks, baby. That was good."

I left him there, watching me, and went to my room before he could tell me to go.

Chapter Eleven
Marcus

"WITH THIS LOCATION and being so close to the water, this property won't last," I told Kurt. He was from New York and was in town on business and looking for a second home out West. I handled both residential and commercial properties, much like my folks did, only they designed and I sold. Kurt was a typical client of mine, someone with a lot of money to spend, some of which would end up in my pocket. I also owned numerous properties of my own throughout LA and San Diego counties and, more recently, in Las Vegas, creating my own empire the way my parents had done.

"It's a little smaller than what I was looking for," Kurt replied.

"It is, but what you lose in square footage, you'll gain in lot size. You won't find many places around here with the extra land space."

I could see the wheels turning in his head because he knew I was right. Now, that didn't mean he would have any use for a bigger lot, but for many, it was a selling point. When he went for the back door and stepped outside to look at the ocean again, I knew I had him. I was good at judging when a client would make an offer and when they wouldn't. I was rarely wrong.

Giving him some space, I stayed inside. I wasn't the kind of man to chase and push for what I wanted from someone, even if that something made me a lot of money...which immediately made me think about Kai. Not the money part, but the not chasing. It had been over a week since we'd sucked each other off and he'd strutted naked out of my room, and...nothing since.

We saw each other, of course, because we lived together. He flirted with me because Kai flirted with everyone, but he hadn't initiated sex again. The little brat basically pretended it didn't happen, and while I should do the same and also shouldn't give a fuck, it was all I could think about. He distracted me, and I didn't like that shit, didn't like having someone on my mind like this. He never stopped finding ways to get under my skin and annoy the hell out of me.

He also seemed to be really moving forward with the Atlanta offer. He'd talked to Declan about it, letting him know that he would be giving notice but would likely be around for another two months or so. And then, despite our conversation about friends, he'd gone out on Friday night.

It doesn't matter. Why do you give a fuck what he's doing? You—

"Mr. Alston?" The way Kurt said my name, I could tell it wasn't the first time.

"Sorry. What did you say?" Motherfucking Kai. I was losing my damn mind.

"You'll be hearing from my agent tonight," Kurt replied.

I smiled. I knew I'd been right about him. At least I hadn't lost that.

"I'm looking forward to it."

I walked him out and then locked up. There were some properties I didn't show myself anymore, but some I knew it was important to handle myself, and this had been one of them. I headed to my car, then straight back to work. When I was finished for the day, I called Corbin.

"What's up, Daddy Marcus?"

"Why do you call me that?"

"Why do you ask me questions when you're never satisfied with my answers?"

He had a point. "Let's grab dinner tonight." Silence greeted me, so I said, "Jesus Christ, Corb. Shut up and have dinner with me."

He laughed. "I didn't even say anything!"

"You didn't have to. I know what you were thinking."

"Well, you have to admit, outside of your home being completely open to us all the time, you're not normally the first one to call and ask one of us to do something. Usually I'm forcing you to be social."

I couldn't say he was wrong. "Don't get used to it."

"Yes, sir. Where are we going?"

"What sounds good to you?"

"Something light."

I rolled my eyes. "We'll do Mediterranean. Meet me at Nil's at six."

"Yes, Daddy."

I groaned but didn't call him on the nickname again.

I made it to Nil's before Corbin did. They seated me, and I pulled out my phone to click on Instagram. First, I checked out the account for Driftwood, which Kai ran for Declan because Declan hated that shit. When I realized I was scrolling and looking for Kai, I nearly threw my phone through the window of the restaurant. I headed to Corbin's page next, which I checked often. There were thirst traps, mirror selfies, workout videos, and photos. Most of the comments were from men telling him how beautiful he was—truth—only they were looking at just what was on the outside and not what actually made Corbin...Corbin. The rest of the comments were from men saying how much they wanted to fuck him, or have Corbin fuck them, talking about his ass or what they wanted to do with his mouth.

Mixed in with all the comments telling Corbin how hot he was and how much they wanted him were three on the last photo that stood out. Two called him full of himself and said he was everything wrong with the queer community, and one said he wasn't even that good-looking. Despite the hundreds of comments saying how beautiful he was, all he would do was focus on those three negative ones. Those were the things about Corbin that no one saw but us. I wished he would just cancel that fucking account altogether, but he never would.

"Sorry I'm late. Why are you stalking me?" Corbin sat down across from me and nodded at my phone.

"Because good Daddies watch their boys' social media activity to make sure they're being appropriate," I joked.

Corbin chuckled. "Being good is no fun."

"Now you sound like Kai," slipped out of my mouth.

He raised a brow, but the waitress stopped by right then and asked if we wanted anything to drink. I wasn't foolish enough to think he wouldn't mention it as soon as she left, but at least it bought me a moment.

"Just water for me," Corbin said, and I told her I'd like the same. I opened my menu when she left, but Corbin wouldn't be deterred. "Mentioning Kai in random conversations now? Didn't Park do that with Elliott in the beginning...and wait...I believe Declan did the same with Sebastian...hmm, curious." I glanced up in time to see him rubbing his chin like he was deep in thought.

"You're an idiot."

"I'm your favorite idiot," he countered. That, I couldn't deny. "Does he happen to have anything to do with your sudden desire to go out to dinner with me?"

"No. I've been going out to dinner with you for a hundred years. I think I'm getting the chicken-kebab platter. You should get the same. You always like that."

"I'm getting a salad. A hundred years, huh?"

"Most of the time it feels that way, yes." When Corbin chuckled, I added, "Get the chicken kebab." I'd chosen it because I knew it was his favorite and what he really wanted. Sometimes Corbin needed a little push to do certain things, like if the choice was taken away from him, he couldn't feel guilty about it.

"Have you hooked up with him yet?"

It was on the tip of my tongue to say no. I wasn't the guy who shared stories about people I slept with. That wasn't how I rolled, but when I opened my mouth, what came out was, "Yes." It was maybe the worst decision I'd ever made in my life, and if I had a time machine, I'd have definitely gone back and changed it.

Corbin's eyes bugged out of his head. "Holy shit. You told me the truth." The waitress dropped our waters off, and when she asked if we were ready to order, Corbin said, "Two chicken-kebab platters."

I told myself that was why I'd admitted to hooking up with Kai, but I was also suddenly a huge fucking liar, even if only to myself. "We blew each other after the dishes one night. That's all you're getting out of me. It's not a thing. He hasn't even mentioned it since." Corbin didn't respond, so I looked at him to see his mouth hanging open dramatically. "I hate you."

"No you don't. You love me…and you like him."

I waved that off. "What the fuck did I just say that told you I like him?"

"Mentioning him at all? And bringing up the fact that he

hasn't said anything about the sex afterward? Oh my God, you're legit offended! The great sexual prowess of Marcus Alston, and Kai has the audacity not to talk about it afterward."

He nearly fell out of his chair laughing. If I had a pillow close, I would have smothered him with it. "I'm done talking about this. How's work?"

"It's okay to like someone, Marcus. Jesus, this feels like déjà vu. One of us said the same shit to Dec."

My stomach twisted up in knots. "This is nothing like Sebastian and Declan. I don't even know the kid."

"Oh, *now* he's a kid because you want to make it sound like you can't possibly like him. I'm not saying you're in love with him or that you know all his deep dark secrets, but he's gotten under your skin, and it's glorious because no one had gotten there before. This is fun." Corbin waggled his brows.

"I'll never ask you to dinner again." But the truth was, I'd known this would happen. There was no doubt in my mind that he would ask because this was Corbin and that's just how we worked. All the Beach Bums did, but especially Corb.

"Marcus," he said softly, with entirely too much emotion in his voice.

"Kid...don't do this. I'm weird about him, but it's not what you think. Maybe it's because he's younger, or because he works with Dec and I know he's important to Dec." I'd never hooked up with someone who was close to my family before. It made perfect sense that it would be the reason I was weird about it. "Also, he's moving, which is a good thing. If he wasn't, I wouldn't have hooked up with him in the first place."

"What?"

I explained the situation with the guy in Atlanta. I was still unsure about it, but Kai wanted me to stay out of it. He'd made his decision.

Corbin sighed. While he liked to push the envelope, he also knew when not to, so instead of asking me more, he said, "I love you, Marcus."

"I love you too, kid." And I did. I loved him, Parker, and Declan. They had never let me down. I never doubted what I meant to them. And on top of that, they made me feel needed. Like I was important to them, like their lives wouldn't be the same without me, and though I'd never told them, I needed that.

"Do we get to talk about the blowjob now?"

"No." I smiled.

"You have to admit it's kinda great that he has you thinking about him like this. I mean, someone who doesn't fall completely under Marcus Alston's control. He's basically a unicorn."

"Oh, I have to admit that, do I?" Jesus, my friends.

"You know this is different."

Thankfully, the waitress brought our food and Corbin got distracted by that. I refused to let myself think about Kai anymore.

Chapter Twelve

Kai

I WAS IN this weird situation where I tried not to think about something I was obsessing about, which only made me think about said thing even more. And by something, I meant *someone*, a.k.a. *Marcus*. It was annoying as shit.

I wasn't the needy, clingy type. That had never been me. It was part of the reason I'd walked out of his room after hooking up, and definitely why I'd given him space over the last eternity, i.e., a little over a week. It was basically the same thing. But it was making me feel antsy, like this extreme case of Marcus-induced FOMO. What if that space made him not want to hook up with me again? Or decide he wanted me to move out early?

But then, what if I went all Kai on him, flirted too much, and he took that as me being clingy, which would have the same effect? I could admit it—sometimes I was basically a tornado in a really sexy, compact body.

So…I decided to do the only thing a man in my situation could do—talk to my boss about it. They were best friends, after all.

Because I knew Declan could be prickly, I decided to wait until the bar closed. What I hadn't expected was Sebastian to come down a little after eleven that night to hide in his corner and spend time with Declan while he worked. That meant I was going to have an audience. A more patient man would've put it off until another night, but I'd never been good at making the smartest decisions.

"Hey, handsome...and hey, equally handsome partner. Did that make sense?"

Declan rolled his eyes, and Sebastian chuckled before saying, "We know what you meant."

Driftwood was empty other than the three of us and one of the security guys, who was there from when we opened until the last employee left for the night, ever since Sebastian had been outed as dating Declan. It wasn't ideal, but better safe than sorry.

"I need your advice," I said, and Declan crossed his arms like he didn't believe me. "What? I'm being serious!"

Declan smirked. "I'm all ears."

Sebastian smirked as well, and rubbed his hands together. "This oughta be good."

"Wow. Your man's excited," I teased, then went straight for it. "So...the Sunday we had the cookout after you guys recorded *The Vers*, Marcus and I hooked up. It was really fucking hot. I mean, he's fine, yeah, but that doesn't mean a guy knows how to—"

"Stop. I'm not all ears anymore." Declan covered them as if he were a child and this would prevent him from hearing me. "I can't talk to you about this."

"Why? Don't the four of you talk about sex all the time? And don't you run a podcast where you talk about this kind of thing and give advice?"

He dropped his arms but didn't respond, probably because he didn't have a good excuse.

"You have to admit he has a point, Dec."

"Thank you, Sebastian."

"Yeah, thanks, Bastian," Declan muttered. "Why am I

suddenly the worst loner ever? I'm not supposed to be the one people go to for stuff like this. Shouldn't you ask Corbin or Parker?"

"I hate to break it to you," Sebastian told him, "but you've always been the worst loner ever."

I grinned. "I love your boyfriend."

"I can't say I'm too happy with him right now," Declan said playfully, making Sebastian laugh. "Fine, finish your question."

"Okay, so we hooked up, and then I left his room before he had the chance to tell me to go. Which is fine. It's not like I think we're boyfriends and wanted him to cuddle and whisper sweet nothings to me all night."

"Cuddling and sweet nothings are the best," Sebastian said, and I was pretty sure Declan melted. He was such a softy and didn't even know it.

"Gross," I joked. "Anyway, ever since, I just acted my usual way around him. I flirt and shit like that because I'm me and I don't really know any other way to be. But I've also done it less and spent less time at home, and I haven't mentioned having sex with him again because I was afraid he'd be all"—I lowered my voice—"*That was a mistake. I don't do love.*" I spoke in my normal voice when I added, "And I'd be all…*Who said anything about love?* And then he'd be all"—I went back to my Marcus voice—"*Yeah, but you're too close, and you're important to Declan. Me stoic man who needs no one, not even good orgasms.* Blah, blah, blah. You get it. You know Marcus. So what should I do?"

They both stood there staring at me as if I'd sprouted another head before busting into laughter.

"Fine. Whatever. I don't need your help. I'll figure it out myself."

I tried to walk away, but Declan eased in front of me to

block my way. "I'm sorry. That was just…interesting, to say the least, and you don't do a bad Marcus impersonation."

"Thanks." I curtsied.

Declan's face morphed from amusement to concern, which basically meant fuck my life. "I don't know what to say. Marcus is my family, and you're important to me. I don't want anyone to get hurt. I know you say you don't want anything serious, but what if you do and Marcus can't give you that? On the flip side, Marcus is different with you, so what if you're his Bastian and turn his whole fucking world upside down, only you're young and not ready to settle down—oh, and moving—and Marcus gets hurt?"

Sebastian wrapped his arms around Declan from behind. "Wow, *swoon*. I love you."

I had to admit, it made my heart go pitter-patter. I couldn't imagine ever feeling for someone the way Sebastian and Declan did for each other…the way my parents did, or my siblings with their spouses. I didn't figure anyone would want to put up with me that long. I cleared my throat. "It's just sex, Declan."

"Yeah, well, Bastian and I were just sex too, and look what happened."

"We're not you two, and as you pointed out, I'm moving."

He sighed, then ran a hand through his dark-blond hair. "Marcus has the biggest heart of anyone I've ever known, but he keeps it behind the thickest wall he can build. I think people sometimes forget or don't realize how much Marcus loves. The ones who hide it the most are the ones who can get hurt more than most people see."

I had no doubt that while Declan was talking about Marcus, he was also speaking from personal experience. My hunch was confirmed when Sebastian kissed his neck in support.

"You think I could hurt Marcus? No offense, but you must have picked up some good stuff at the dispensary because someone like him would never fall for someone like me."

Sebastian frowned, and Declan's brows pulled together. "Marcus would be lucky to have someone like you, Kai, just like you would be to have him. Don't put yourself down."

Wow. Declan was being all sorts of open tonight. "Okay, sure, in theory, but it's not going to happen."

"Coming at this from another angle, then, we can focus on those big, thick walls I mentioned."

"We're getting off-track here. I just wanted your opinion on trying to hook up with him again, or if I should be waiting until he comes to me." Marcus was…extremely out of my league, and I wasn't dumb enough to think otherwise. Sex was totally different from all the stuff Declan was talking about.

"I think you're strong and independent. You're going to do what you want and what you think is best regardless of what I say—and I'm not telling you that's a bad thing."

I watched him for a moment, unsure how to take what he said, then decided to lighten the mood. "You're no help at all, Declan. Maybe I should message *The Vers*."

Declan barked out a laugh. "Go home, Kai. I'll finish up here."

"You two are going to have sex here, aren't you?" I teased.

He smiled and shook his head. "Go home."

"Don't have to tell me twice."

I made it all the way to the door before Declan said, "Hey, Kai?"

"Yeah?"

"Marcus took you to his room when you hooked up?"

I nodded. "Why?"

"Just curious."

I shrugged and headed out, still debating what I was going to do.

When I got home, I was surprised to find Marcus awake and looking at the fish tank. Considering it was almost three in the morning, I didn't usually run into him after work.

"I think Blue is sick."

My heart dropped. "What? Are you serious?" I raced over to the tank to see my blue tang floating close to the bottom, hiding toward the back.

"I checked the water. All your levels are perfect. The temperature is right; the salt levels are on target." I was obsessive about my tank and checked everything twice a week. I'd done it myself two days ago, and everything was good then as well. "I looked it up and saw you're feeding them high-quality frozen food."

It was cute how Marcus was doing this kind of research, but I kept that to myself. "They're unusual fish in general. They can act a little goofy, but…Blue's color looks slightly off. I should go get another tank in the morning. If Blue's sick, we don't want to risk the other fish."

I watched Blue roll over on his side before floating upright again. That wasn't necessarily cause for alarm because blue tangs were weird, but together with the color being off…something wasn't right.

We both watched the tank for a few minutes, quietly. My stomach was twisted up with worry, and I was relieved he got it; most people wouldn't understand. "I know it seems stupid to be so worried about a fish, but…taking care of them feels good. I can be a little wild, but they always soothe me. I feel like I let Blue down if they're sick." I tried to use *they* for my fish.

Marcus didn't respond for what felt like a hundred years. When I turned to look at him, he was watching me, questions in his eyes I couldn't read but still had no doubt were there.

"Get some sleep, Kai. I'll stay up and watch them. When the stores open, I'll go get a tank or whatever you need. We'll make sure Blue's okay. You're doing good by them."

I had to admit, it was adorable that Marcus used *they* now too for my fish.

And it meant a lot to me that he took this seriously. That he didn't roll his eyes or think I was being extra over a damn fish.

"You have to be up early for work, Marcus. You should try and go to bed. I can stay up and go to the store in the morning. They're my responsibility, not yours."

"Stubborn little thing, aren't you?"

"Stubborn big thing, aren't you?" I countered.

Marcus sighed, closed his eyes, and shook his head. It wasn't in the same way that some people did when they were exhausted with me. Without a word, he walked over to the small love seat and stood at one end. "You gonna help me with this or what?"

Inexplicably, my heart sped. "What are we doing?" I walked over to him.

"Moving this."

Oh. I took the other end, Marcus and I pulling the couch over so it was in front of the tank. He was only wearing a pair of basketball shorts, low on his hips, and from the lack of a band and the way his cock swung, totally free-balling it.

"Go get changed, Kai."

I nodded, a little dumbfounded.

I hurried upstairs, cleaned up a bit, and changed into a pair of shorts. When I got back downstairs, Marcus was sitting on the couch with a bottle of wine and slider sandwiches.

When he looked at me, I couldn't help smiling. Who knew *The Vers*'s realist was secretly the sweetest man in the world.

Chapter Thirteen
Marcus

"SIT. EAT," I said as Kai stood at the bottom of the stairs, watching me. His lips stretched into a mischievous grin. "You're so damn ornery."

"I didn't even do anything," he replied before adding, "Yes, sir," and walking over.

I cocked a brow. He'd just proven my point. "I'm waiting for the punchline. Nothing is ever this simple with you."

Kai crossed his arms. "I'm easy."

"Yeah, okay. And I'm sweet and fluffy."

"You *are* sweet and fluffy, Marcus. You just refuse to see it. Now, I'm gonna go get some water because I'm not bougie enough for wine. Then I'll do exactly as Daddy says."

I rolled my eyes, but it wasn't until he was in the kitchen behind me that I realized I was smiling. I bit down on my cheek and forced myself to school my features. Considering it was the middle of the night and we were staying up to watch a damn fish as if there was anything we could do, there was no reason for me to be grinning.

Kai got his drink and set it on the coffee table, which I'd also moved over while he was upstairs. When he sat, he did so right next to me, our legs touching. "Wine is bougie?" I asked.

"Either that, or it's for old people." He winked, plucked one of the sliders from the plate, and took a bite.

"You better be playin'," I told him, but Kai just shrugged. "You're twenty-six. Nine years doesn't make me old."

He gave a ridiculous snort-laugh that shouldn't be cute, but it was. "Funny that you say those words because I guarantee if I was like, *Hey, date me, Marcus*—I'm not saying that, by the way—but if I were, and even if you wanted the same thing, you'd be like, *I'm too old for you.*"

"No I wouldn't," I lied. Hell, I'd probably already mentioned his age in one way or another, and if I hadn't, I'd thought about it.

"Oh my God. Shut the fuck up. You're so full of shit."

"Eat your food," I said again.

"Does that always work for you? Changing the subject by being bossy? Or just being bossy twenty-four seven?"

"Have you met Corbin, Parker, and Declan? It never works."

Kai chuckled. "Good point." He picked up a slider. "If I have to eat, you do too." He handed it over, and I didn't argue. "So what are you doing up anyway?"

"Couldn't sleep. Happens sometimes."

"That sucks. I can always sleep—anytime, anywhere. What did you do today?"

"Worked, then had dinner at a Mediterranean restaurant with Corbin. Went for a jog when I got home, then did some admin work."

It was strange talking like this about my day. Even when I was growing up, my folks didn't really do this. Since they worked together, they knew what the other had been up to. And if not, it was more professional than conversational. Kai was asking because he wanted to check on me, not on work things. Because that's what most people did.

He continued to ask questions, and I continued to answer while we finished the food and drinks. When the plate was empty, he rubbed his stomach. "I'm stuffed."

His shirt lifted up, showing me his flat abs. I wanted to lick each one of them before my mouth found its way down to his cock again.

Kai swatted my thigh. "Not that kind of stuffed. Get your mind out of the gutter."

"Whose mind is in the gutter? Because that's not what I was thinking."

"Who knew you lied so much?" He smiled before his gaze drifted to the tank. "I hope Blue is okay. As I said, it's important to me to take good care of them. Not just because they're living, breathing creatures—clearly, that too—but because... I guess because I always worried I wouldn't be able to take care of myself, much less someone else. But then I moved to Santa Monica, and while it might be a struggle, I'm doing my thing and I'm taking care of them." Kai leaned against the back of the couch and put his feet on the table. "Stupid, huh?"

"Not stupid. There's nothing wrong with wanting to be independent and wanting to do well. And there's nothing wrong with loving your fish. They might not be okay, but that's not your fault. We all get sick sometimes, and eventually, we'll all die." I looked at him, and he had his nose crinkled up.

"Not helping, baby. How about no realism tonight? Blue will be perfectly fine! No one dies, ever."

"You know what I mean." I filled my wineglass before leaning back beside him. "What are all their names?"

He went through each one and told me about them and how long he'd had them. They meant a lot to him, and I damn sure hoped Blue would be okay. Kai would take it personally if they weren't, and I didn't want him to feel as if he'd done something wrong. "Is that why you didn't want to move back to Riverside? What you said about taking care of yourself?"

He nodded. "My family is great. I'm the baby. My parents both worked full-time jobs to make ends meet, and my siblings helped out with me a lot. Jalen is the oldest. He's the first person I told I'm gay."

"It went well, I take it."

"Oh yeah. I was young, but I knew I was different, and I knew that difference wasn't okay with everyone, but it would be with my family. We stick together and always have each other's backs. He was like…*That's cool, little man. You know I love you, right?* And when I said yeah, he told me if anyone fucks with me, to tell him, but he also started teaching me how to take care of myself. I might not look like it, but I'm a bad motherfucker."

Kai grinned, and I laughed. There was something infectious about him that made me feel…well, not like me. "You look like a bad motherfucker."

"Thank you." He dropped his head to my shoulder. "Anyway…Faith is my sister. I told her next, and it went just like it had with Jalen. They sat down with me when I told my parents. Even though they worked a lot, they always made sure all five of us sat down at the table together for dinner at least a few times a week. I was always a ball of energy, but even more that day, bouncing around in my seat before blurting out that I was gay. Mom and Dad just looked at me for a minute, and my heart seized up. I thought I'd gotten it wrong and they weren't going to be okay, but Mama was like, *We know, baby. Can you pass the mashed potatoes?* And that was that."

I chuckled, thinking about a young Kai sitting at a table with his family, the laughter and conversation. "Sounds nice."

"Shit. I'm sorry. I didn't mean…"

I waved off his concern. "Nah, it is what it is. I don't let myself worry about things I can't change. And fuck, in a lot of ways, I was lucky. I grew up in a two-parent home. We never had to worry about where rent money would come from. My parents worked their asses off to be successful, and I respect the shit out of them for it. They instilled a strong work ethic in me and taught me to be proud of who I am—as a gay man *and* as a Black man." But there was a time I wished I had what Kai did—laughter and family dinners.

"I bet you were an overachiever."

I turned my head, and Kai looked up at me. "What was your first clue?" I asked sarcastically.

"Be nice."

"I am being nice," I said, then, "my parents had high standards. I couldn't get anything below an A. I was in every fucking activity you can think of—music, art, languages. They wanted me to have what they'd lacked growing up. I don't want to sound like they were cold or didn't love me. I just... If they asked *how was your day*, they meant what did you accomplish, and because of that, I have all this." And how could I ever complain about the situation I was in? That my parents defied the odds and created an empire?

"I don't think they were cold." And then...then Kai slipped his arm through mine, hooking them together before laying his head on my shoulder again. "When I ask how your day was, I don't care what you accomplished, though, okay? I want to know about stuff in here." He patted my chest, right above my heart, and that touch somehow sucked the air out of me. I didn't know what to say, how to respond, or why I suddenly *felt* so fucking much.

I cleared my throat, trying to ignore what he'd said. My brain wouldn't obey, but my mouth did. "You never fully answered my question—if that's why you don't want to go back to Riverside. We ended up talking about when you came out."

"Oh yeah. It's hard because, like you, I'm so fucking lucky to have them. They're my world, but I've always been different from them too. Faith went to college to be a nurse. Jalen did an apprenticeship to be an electrician. I did nothing. I got a job, yeah, but our paths are different. They both settled down young, the way our parents did. I'm twenty-six, and I've never brought a man home. I need my space to be who I am. And sometimes I feel like they think they have to take care of me. I'm too irresponsible or wild or whatever. I'm sure that sounds silly—"

"Nah. I get it. It's similar to me and why even though I have a degree in architecture, I went into real estate. There's nothing wrong with wanting to stand on your own two feet."

"Exactly…and wow…I have something in common with Marcus Alston. Go me."

I chuckled, and then we both turned quiet for a moment. My wineglass was still full on the table in front of us, the fish swimming, except for Blue, who was lingering toward the bottom, alternating between staying upright and lying down. There was something peaceful about them, which was why I'd ended up downstairs watching them—and that's how I realized Blue wasn't acting normal in the first place.

I frowned when Kai untangled himself from me, saying, "I'll be right back," but all he did was get up and turn off the lights in the room before joining me again. "How did you guys start *The Vers*?"

"We can blame that completely on Corbin and Parker. They dragged Dec and me kicking and screaming. We got lucky that it ended up being profitable. Most podcasts aren't. I kept telling Corbin that from the beginning. It's all about sponsors and advertisers."

"But even if it didn't make money, it would be fun, no? You get to do something with your best friends."

"Is that supposed to be good?" I teased, then added, "Yeah, it would be."

"I know. Tell me something else."

So that's what I did. Kai curled up against me, and I talked... He interrupted a lot, and my stories turned into his stories, but I was okay with that. The night went on, the two of us in the dark other than the light from the tank, just sharing with each other.

Eventually, his voice started to go hoarse, and I could tell he was getting tired. He'd been working all night, so it made sense he was exhausted. "Go to sleep, baby boy."

"You're not the boss of me," he said, but when I wrapped my arm around him, Kai nuzzled in and almost immediately passed out.

Chapter Fourteen

Kai

I WOKE UP to the heat of another body wrapped around mine, warm and hard with muscles covered in smooth skin.

I didn't know how it happened, but we were lying down now, both of us on our sides, with Marcus behind me, his arm around my waist and a very thick erection nuzzling against my ass.

I couldn't complain. It might just be the best way I'd ever woken up.

As I was about to push back against him, I remembered the whole reason we were cuddled up on the couch and scrambled over to the tank to look at my fish. Blue didn't look better, but they didn't look worse either.

"Shit. I can't believe I slept in," Marcus's deep voice came from behind me.

"Slow your roll there, big guy. It's eight. In what world is this sleeping in?"

I turned to him. He was sitting up now, rubbing a hand over his face.

"Mine."

"Your world is weird."

He looked at me, a strange smile on his face I couldn't read. "Let's get dressed so we can go get stuff taken care of."

"Is this getting-dressed thing something we're doing

together? I could handle a shower together too. I'll grab my stuff and meet you in your room." I waggled my brows, Marcus shook his head at me, but he loved this shit. I stirred up his life, and he needed that.

"Be good, baby boy." He stood.

"How am I supposed to be good when you call me that? All it makes me want to do is have sex with you." Shit. Well, I guess I wasn't playing hard to get anymore. It had lasted barely over a week, but I was surprised I'd made it this long.

He didn't respond, instead walking over to look at Blue, which made me feel guilty for wanting to have an orgasm instead of taking care of them.

"I was kidding. I'm gonna go get dressed. You have to work today. You really don't need to come with me. I can handle it."

"Did I say you couldn't?" He headed for the stairs. "I emailed my assistant and let her know I'd be taking the day off."

He had? For me? I couldn't make sense of it. All I was doing was getting stuff to transfer Blue to another tank and hoping the people at the fish store had some ideas on how I could make sure they'd be okay. While it was important to me, there was no reason for it to be important to Marcus. There was also no reason he had to go with me, even though it was sweet.

"Marcus," I said when he got to the bottom of the stairs, and he turned to look at me. "Thank you...for everything."

He shrugged as if it wasn't a big deal. "Nothing to thank me for."

But really there was. On the other hand, Marcus got something out of this too. I thought...hell, I thought maybe he needed to feel needed. That this man who was so confident, beautiful, successful, and basically perfect, put himself out there for others, did things for them because it was how he felt wanted and important.

For the first time in my life, I *felt* my heart doing something funny, like it was physically softening, which was weird and something I definitely planned to bury and ignore.

I went to my room, took the world's fastest shower, and got dressed. Marcus was already waiting for me in the living room when I got there.

My breath caught in my throat when I saw him. He was wearing a pair of jeans and a tight, black V-neck tee that hugged his strong arms and defined pecs like a glove. He needed to clean up his shave, but it didn't take away from how fine Marcus Alston was. When you added in his heart? Well, he'd make someone very happy one day.

"We can take my car," he said, pulling me from my thoughts, and grabbed a pair of sunglasses.

"Bet. Let me get some photos and video of Blue first."

"I did while you were upstairs."

Oh. Wow. He thought of everything.

I grabbed my shit too and went to Marcus's BMW with him. Like I'd been taught to do, he also put his wallet and ID on the dashboard so he could reach them easily if needed. It didn't matter that in some ways Marcus and I were complete opposites and had different experiences in life. Some of our experiences as Black men were universal.

When he pulled out of the driveway, I rolled my window down some. The September weather in Santa Monica was perfect, not that it wasn't always. We averaged low 70s this time of year and about twenty days of rain a year. I couldn't imagine why anyone would want to live anywhere else. The temperature was definitely something I would miss when I moved to Atlanta…

To distract myself, I asked Marcus, "Are you going

through withdrawal?"

He glanced at me from behind his sunglasses. "From sex with you? We only had it once."

I laughed. "Um...no, I meant from work, but I guess that applies as well." His mouth opened on a small O, like he couldn't believe he'd said that, which made me crack up even more. "Looks like someone has my body on their mind."

"No I don't."

"Okay, Mr. Realist. Isn't part of your persona that you're totally honest? Methinks you are a big, huge liar."

It was his turn to chuckle, rich and deep in that way only Marcus did. "Fine. Then yes."

"To which question?"

He gave me a surprisingly playful grin. "Both."

"Wow...so you miss having orgasms with me as much as you miss going to work." I clutched my chest. "Be still my heart. That's a Southern saying, right? I'm supposed to say stuff like that when I live in Atlanta."

"Guess so."

"Well...just so you know...I'm going through withdrawal too. It's been killing me to be good. I even got advice from Declan last night."

"Aw, shit. I'm never gonna hear the end of it now."

"I'm pretty sure I've heard a story about you busting Corbin out of a cock-cage-gone-wrong incident. You guys share everything."

"I don't share everything. Corbin shares everything. Parker shares most things. Declan shares more now."

If I'd thought he would really be upset, I never would have said anything, but still, I turned his way and asked, "Should I really not have?" Just to make sure. The last thing I wanted was to put Marcus's private business on blast.

"It's Declan. It's fine." When I smiled, he added, "Shut

up."

"I didn't say a word."

"You didn't have to."

We chatted and joked around while we drove to the fish store. He seemed a little more open around me than he used to be, like he'd let some of his guard down. I didn't figure Marcus ever let all his defenses down with anyone, not even the Beach Bums, so I was honored he'd given me some.

There were only a couple of people in the fish store when we arrived, thankfully, since we'd gotten there so early. I went right up to one of the employees, with Marcus beside me. He was a hoverer, I'd noticed, which was both surprising and amazing.

"Can I help you?" the woman asked.

"Yeah, we have a blue tang, and I think they're sick. I'm going to get the stuff to transfer them to another tank so we don't risk the other fish, but I wanted to see if you have any other suggestions."

"I took some video of how they've been acting compared to the others," Marcus added. He pulled his phone out and showed the woman the footage he'd taken.

"Any changes for them?"

"I moved a couple of weeks ago. I considered that, but I figured if that was the problem, they would have acted differently right away."

"Yes and no. Or maybe you didn't notice. There are a lot of things it could be. It's definitely smart to separate them. It could be bacterial as well. Oh, yep, look. You see those small white spots? It looks like it might have Ich."

She said that as if I should know, but I'd never heard of it. When she went to get what I needed for it, I told Marcus, "I feel like a bad fish daddy. I don't even know what that is."

"You're not a bad fish daddy," he said, and when our

gazes caught, we burst into laughter. It wasn't every day I heard someone like Marcus say *fish daddy*. I wished he'd say it again so I could record him. When he settled down, he said, "It's impossible to know every little thing it could be. Everyone gets sick."

"Yes, I know. You already went all realist on me and told me that eventually my fish will die."

"Stop being a little monster. I'm just saying don't feel bad."

"I have a feeling if the situation were reversed and these were your fish, you would. You hold yourself to different standards than everyone else."

"Yes." He shrugged as if that was perfectly normal. "See? I don't lie."

The woman came back with a medication bottle and explained how to use it. Marcus asked questions because that was how Marcus was. Eventually, I left him to it while I started picking out the things I needed for another small tank. It wasn't going to be cheap, which stressed me out. This was the hard part of living in a place like Santa Monica. I was living paycheck to paycheck, so the smallest thing could set me back. I looked forward to that not being the case in Atlanta.

Marcus joined me as I was making my way to the counter, too much in my arms. He took some of it while I showed them which tank I wanted. I'd also purchased salt water, so there were several five-gallon jugs waiting for me. When they gave me the total, I felt his gaze on me, knew he wanted to offer to help, and I appreciated that he didn't, knowing it was just because he knew I wouldn't want that.

"Thank you," I said as we made our way outside.

"For what?"

"I know how hard that was for you, so…thank you."

"I don't know what you're talking about," he replied, but we both knew he did.

"Liar, liar, pants on fire."

"Get in the car."

"Yes, Daddy."

He rolled his eyes at me like he so often did. He put all the supplies in, and then we returned to his house. We spent the morning setting up the new tank, getting it warm, testing levels and all. No matter how many times I told Marcus he didn't have to help, he continued to. It was after lunch when we had Blue in the new tank, having treated both tanks to kill the bacteria. None of the other fish seemed to be affected yet, but they very well could be soon.

When we were finished, I told him, "I'm making you lunch. And then we're going to play in the ocean." He already took the day off, so why not?

"No."

"Yes."

"No," he countered again.

"I don't know why you pretend to argue with me, baby." Because the truth was, Marcus might want to be gruff, but there wasn't anything he wouldn't do for anyone. He proved it with his friends daily—not that I saw myself on the same level as them.

"Can you even cook?"

"I'm gonna act like you didn't say that." I went into the kitchen. "I love to cook. I was always cooking with my mama. I might not have been to the South, but I love me some soul food. Chicken and waffles work?"

"I'm getting my laptop," Marcus answered.

"No! You said you're taking the day off. You leave this room, and I'll tackle you."

"I've been working with you all morning." He quirked a

brow.

"That's different. It's not your job. If you walk out of this room, Marcus Alston, I'll jump on your back and stay there all day."

He crossed his arms. "I don't think you realize people don't talk to me like that."

"Yes. So you've told me before, but *I* do." I pointed to a chair. He walked over and sat in a different one, smirking. I couldn't help but roll my eyes. Still, I loved this version of Marcus.

We talked while I pulled out all the ingredients and started whipping up my mama's recipe. He didn't speak as much as me, but he didn't work and he didn't walk away either.

The food was perfect, both the waffles and the chicken a golden brown I had to admire for a moment because I was proud of it. I handed him a plate and nodded toward the door. "Outside?"

Marcus shrugged but went with me.

The sound of the ocean danced along the air as we sat outside, eating our food. "Fuck...good, right?" I asked around a bite.

"I can't complain. Who knew you had it in you?"

"I'm ignoring that. Cooking was always how we brought the family together, whether it was cookouts or all of us piling around the table to eat. When we were having a bad day, my mama would take us out to ice cream, even if we couldn't really afford it. Both my folks would sacrifice what they needed for us. Kinda how you do with your friends."

He frowned as he finished chewing. "I don't do that."

"There you go being a liar again." I smiled. "When I was a kid, I woke my folks up with breakfast in bed every birthday, Mother's Day, Father's Day, and shit like that. Food is amazing for bringing people together."

"Why is this the first time you've cooked since you've been here?"

I shrugged. "It's your house. You always grill when your friends are here. I didn't want to intrude."

"You live here, Kai. You're not intruding."

I trembled, his words washing over me. "It's hot when you say my name."

"Be good."

"You're always telling me that."

"You never listen," he countered.

"Because you don't really want me to." I scooped another sweet bite into my mouth, and Marcus turned his attention back to his food too.

We sat there together after we finished eating. The afternoon passed faster than it felt like it should. He told me more about his work, the houses he was showing, and how much real estate he had—sometimes renting, sometimes selling, but they were all revenue streams for him.

"You should be proud of yourself, Marcus. I love seeing anyone succeed, but it's extra special when it's people who look like me."

"I started out with more than a lot of people."

"That doesn't diminish what you've accomplished. You worked for it the same way as your parents worked for it…the same Jalen did with his electrician program or Faith did in nursing school." I felt really fucking behind right then, but I reminded myself that I would be moving to Atlanta soon, getting my own place and managing what would be a very popular gay bar. That was something. When he didn't respond, I said, "Let's go swimming."

"You were serious about that?"

"You live on the beach, Marcus! We're taking advantage!" I pushed to my feet, took his hand, and pulled him up.

We went inside to change. Marcus had a cabinet for towels outside, so we grabbed some before making our way to the gate that led to the sand.

There were people down the beach in the distance, but no one close. We laid our towels out, and then I took his hand again. "We're just going to run and dive in."

"Are we suddenly twelve?"

"No. We're fun. On the count of three. One…"

"This is dumb."

"Two…"

"I swear you're like a younger version of Corbin."

"Three!" I said, and he didn't hold back. Marcus ran with me, water splashing up our legs until we were deep enough to dive in. It was cold as shit, and the second I broke the surface, I was shivering.

"Wow, you big baby," he said, clearly able to tell. I was about to tell him to fuck off, but then he grabbed me and pulled me into his arms, and oh, it was very, very nice there.

Chapter Fifteen
Marcus

I DIDN'T KNOW how Kai was able to get me to do half the things he did. I just...did them. Yeah, I argued and pretended I wasn't going to, but I always gave in and likely knew from the start I would.

"Mmm, this is nice, baby," he said as I squeezed him tight. He was trembling, his body getting used to the water. While yes, he was sexy as fuck and I wanted to touch him, I had ulterior motives too. As he nuzzled in, getting comfortable, the waves pushing us along, I dunked him, keeping ahold and pulling him up again. "You asshole! That was cheating! I was distracted by your body!"

"Whose fault is that?" I countered, and then...then I played around with him the same way I would with Corbin, Parker, and Declan. We stayed out there for a while before making our way to the towels again. The afternoon was starting to cool off—well, at least for us. The 60s was basically sweater-weather, so we ended up at my firepit, red and yellow flames dancing in front of us.

Kai said, "Can I ask you a personal question?"

"Those are my least favorite kind of questions," I replied, which made him chuckle.

"That's not a no, so I'm going to ask anyway. You and Corbin...has there ever been anything there?"

I wasn't surprised that's what he wanted to know because a lot of people did and were typically disappointed in my answer. "Nope. Never. I know that's hard for people to understand. All three of them are my brothers. Is it a little different with Corb? Yes. Maybe it's because we met first. We were kids, no one knowing all the parts of us when we started talking online. He opened up to me, and…fuck…it felt good to be there for him." But more than that… "He was the first person I ever felt like they needed me, like I was important to them. He made me feel less alone when I still gave a shit about things like that."

Kai sucked in a breath, and I realized what I'd said. It was like he had some kind of magic, and I fell under his spell every time. It lured out my secrets, comforted me, and if I let my guard down, I feared there was nothing he couldn't get me to say. "Do you think he's in love with you?" Kai asked. "I don't listen to *The Vers* often, but I've heard stories and seen the way you two are with each other."

"No. He's not in love with me either, but he needs me. I don't know why, but I'm not sure the why of it matters. All three of them will always be a part of my life, but Corbin is my heart, in the most platonic way possible."

"Damn…I can't imagine having someone say something like that about me. Hopefully your future boyfriend isn't the jealous type."

I almost asked if *he* was the jealous type, but I bit back the question because it didn't matter. Kai was temporarily my roommate, and we'd sucked each other off once. That was the extent of it. "I have no plans to have one of those, but if I did, he would have to understand." Because I could never turn my back on my friends. They were ridiculous and more times than not annoyed the shit out of me, but they were mine.

"I like you, Marcus," Kai said, making my head whip

around so fast, it nearly gave me whiplash. "Don't lose your shit. Not like *that*. I'm just saying you're special, and believe me, I know special because I am too."

I chuckled, but the thing was, I agreed with Kai—about him, not me. "You hungry?" I asked instead of responding to what he'd said.

"Yep, but you're not cooking for me. I'm making dinner. We can check on Blue, and I'll find something to throw together for us. I'm taking care of you for a change."

There was no stopping Kai when he got something in his head, but still I told him, "You don't have to do that."

"I want to. Or we can cook together." He jumped up, grabbed my wrist, and tugged me to my feet. "Let's go."

"Give me a second. I have to put the fire out."

"Hurry. I'll see what we have."

He left, and damned if he wasn't shaking his ass on purpose. I smiled because it was such a Kai thing to do.

I extinguished the fire, then used the outdoor shower to rinse off, tugging my trunks off too and hanging them before wrapping a towel around my waist.

Kai was in the kitchen, wearing a T-shirt and a pair of underwear. Heat rushed to my groin because damn, he had a fine ass. I wanted inside it.

"Are you naked under there?"

I didn't consider telling him no, or that it didn't matter. There were no jokes on my tongue or the urge to tell him to be good while I went and got dressed. The truth was, I didn't want to be good...or under control. Maybe it was just how much I enjoyed today, but I was tired of being so measured, of denying myself what I wanted—him. "Come over and find out."

His pupils flared, and a smile tugged at his lips. Kai closed the fridge and came over, stopping when our toes were touching. The scent of soap tickled my nose, so he must have taken a quick shower before I came in. "I'm not so hungry for food anymore."

I crossed my arms and leaned against the counter. "What are you hungry for?"

"You." Kai reached over and pulled on my towel, making it come free and dropping it to the floor. My cock was already hard—tall and pointing up at him.

"Kiss it," I said, to see if he'd listen.

Kai knelt and pressed his lips to my thigh. "Right here?" Looking down at him, I shook my head. He went to my other leg and did the same. "Here?"

"You always have to be ornery, don't you?"

"It's a talent." I didn't respond, and Kai kept his gaze trained up at me as he leaned in and kissed my full sac. My dick twitched.

"Closer," I told him.

"Ah, right here, then?" And with that, he finally pressed his lips to the head of my cock. All sorts of filthy words wanted to fall out of my mouth at the simple contact. Kai got in my head, under my skin, in ways I'd never experienced. A torrent of need washed over me.

"Upstairs. Supplies are in my room." I didn't *have* to take him upstairs to fuck him. There were condoms and lube in the spare downstairs, which was usually where I hooked up. He always made me make bad decisions, though.

Kai stood and surprised me by taking my hand. "Let's go, baby. I'll take care of you up there, then come down to feed you."

I allowed Kai to lead me to my room. The second we were inside, I pulled out of his hold. "Take your clothes off." He went for his underwear, but I shook my head. "Shirt first."

"I see how this is gonna go." Kai gave me a flirty grin but

obeyed. I stroked my cock while I watched him, and he whimpered after tugging the shirt over his head and dropping it. "God, you're so fucking hot."

"So are you. Now the bottoms."

For the second time, Kai did as I said, removing them, his erection springing free. I stepped closer to him and cupped his tight balls, which were filled with his load. "I can't wait to empty these with my dick deep inside you. Are you gonna give me your hole?"

"Fuck." His eyes rolled back. "You know I am. I've been dying for you to take it."

"That's what I want to hear," I said just before my mouth came down on his in a hard kiss. My tongue pushed its way into his mouth, sweeping in before I eased back some and bit his lip. "I love the taste of these." I traced first his bottom lip, then his top one with my tongue before kissing him again. Kai melted against me, arms around me, blunt nails digging into my back. I swear it was like he tried to fucking climb me, arms and legs seeking, but I didn't give him what he wanted, holding him in place because I could, and we both liked it.

When he reached for my dick, I held his wrists, not willing to give Kai what he wanted yet.

"Bastard," he said when my mouth trailed down his neck.

"Not the first time I've heard that, and it won't be the last." I smiled, then bit gently into the meaty part of his shoulder.

"Jesus, you're killing me. I'm about to bust out of my skin here."

"Ask me," I told him, moving to the other side of his throat.

"Fuck me, Marcus," he begged, making my cock flex against my stomach.

"Turn around." I stepped back, dick leaking and dying to

do exactly what Kai asked me to do. "Bend over the bed and let me see that ass."

I ignored him while I plucked the lube and a condom from the drawer, tossing them to the mattress before seeing Kai in position. I moved behind him, grazing my hand over his ass cheeks and watching as goose bumps followed. It really was a great ass. Holding out this long had been a miracle.

My fingers danced their way up his back next, his brown skin pebbling there too. "I'm going to wreck you."

"Promises, promises," he replied, making laughter jump from my mouth. "Can you get to it now?" He wiggled his ass.

I spread his cheeks, looked down at his tight pucker. "I want a little taste first." I waited for a moment to make sure he was fine with it.

"Fuck yes. I love having my ass eaten."

"Good thing I'm the best at it." I dropped down behind him, again spreading his pert cheeks. A shiver ran the length of Kai, and for a moment, I swear it went from him into me. "You want my tongue?" I circled my finger around his rim.

"You know I do."

"Not as much as I want your hole," I replied, leaning in and tasting him.

"Fuck yes," Kai moaned as I went to town on him, licking and kissing, tasting and savoring his salt-and-soap-flavored skin. He pushed back against me, riding my face like he couldn't get enough of me. The thing was, I couldn't get enough of him either. I kept trying to soften him up, hardened my tongue as I worked to get it inside his tight ring. "Don't stop," Kai said when I pulled back.

"I'm not going anywhere, baby boy. Just going to finger-fuck you for a minute before I eat your hole again."

"Hurry. I'm impatient when I'm horny."

"So basically all the time?" I teased before sucking a finger into my mouth and then pushing at him. I watched his body open up for me, saw it suck my digit inside, which was one of the sexiest fucking things I'd ever seen. Kai was tight and hot, squeezing me like he was made for me.

Pushing deeper, I quirked my finger and rubbed his prostate, chuckling when his knee gave out before he forced it to lock again.

"Add another finger."

"I thought you wanted my tongue?"

"Another finger and then your tongue."

It sounded like a perfect idea to me, but still I said, "Only if you ask nicely."

"I hate you. Fuck me with two fingers, *please*," he begged again, making me laugh.

"Since you asked so politely."

I did exactly as he wanted, sneaking two fingers into the tight glove of his body. Kai's hands fisted in the blanket, his ass practically following my hand, needing more. When I pulled my fingers out, I watched him stay open for me just before I pushed my tongue inside.

"*Goddamn*, I love this," he said, and I did too. I could feast on his ass all fucking night, but my dick was aching to be inside him. My whole body was primed, like all it would take was the smallest push before I fell over the edge.

I shoved to my feet.

"How do you want me?" he asked.

"Just like that with your ass in the air." I smacked it, the sound echoing through the room. I suited up, rolling the rubber down my cock before pumping lube into my hand and slicking up myself and then Kai's hole. Holding the base of my shaft, with my crown at his rim, I said, "Tell me what you want."

"Goddamn you, Marcus!" Kai tried to push back and

impale himself on my cock.

"So naughty. Just tell me what you want."

"Your cock."

"What about it?"

"Give me your fucking cock before I die."

Laughter bubbled up inside me, but I managed to hold it back. "All you had to do was ask." I slowly worked my way into him. My dick was a whole lot thicker than my two fingers, but Kai took it. His body opened up for me, accepted me, was fucking hungry for me, and I wanted nothing more than to give him what he craved.

"Christ, you're big."

"Need me to stop?" I asked when I was about halfway in.

"Nah, I'm good. Jerk me off."

Wrapping my hand around him, I stroked his prick while continuing to give him small thrusts, each time pushing farther and farther into him.

"Fuck...yes...keep going," he said, and I did, until Kai just pushed back, taking the rest of what he wanted.

I almost came.

Right.

Then.

I pulled back and snapped my hips forward, fucking him. My hands moved to his hips now, holding him in place, and I wondered if my fingers would leave bruises there. When I loosened my grip, Kai said, "Tighter," and I listened, squeezing him as I took the ass he gave me.

The room was filled with sounds of sex and breathing, our bodies slapping together. Kai took over jacking himself as I did my best to wreck him the way I promised.

My balls were so fucking full. I didn't know how much longer I could last, but then his ass spasmed around me. Kai tensed and said my name as his body jerked and he shot all over my bed. My orgasm came right behind his, my release filling the condom.

He fell to the bed, and I went down beside him as Kai said, "That was...holy fuck, that was fucking bomb."

"Bomb?" I grabbed a pillow and smashed it into his face before standing and heading into the en suite to get rid of the condom and clean up. I came back with a wet washcloth and tossed it to him.

"What, you're not going to clean me off?" He fluttered his lashes playfully but took care of the mess himself.

"Too late now."

"Ugh. Fine. I'm still going to cook for you."

I nodded. "Okay." He tugged his underwear on, then looked at me. I couldn't read his expression, and hell, I wasn't sure I knew what I was thinking either as I said, "We'll cook together."

"Okay."

"And this... If you want, we can keep doing this until you leave."

Kai smiled so wide, I swear it almost knocked me on my ass. I nearly felt the damn thing, like walking out and feeling the sun on your skin after being cold. "Oh, baby, I so want that. Funny how you thought you might not."

I rolled my eyes, but he was right.

Chapter Sixteen

Kai

"I STILL CAN'T believe you'd rather live with a strange man than your own family," Mama said while we were on the phone. Marcus was at work, and I was off and sitting outside by his pool. It had been a couple of days since he'd gone to the fish store with me. Blue was thankfully doing better, and no one else had gotten sick. Marcus adorably checked on them multiple times a day. I'd caught him watching the fish.

He'd fucked me once more since then too, but we actually didn't have a lot of time together. I worked four days a week but went in late and worked late too, so by the time I got up, he was gone, and by the time I got home, he was asleep.

"He's not a strange man. He's my boss's best friend." When she didn't respond, I added, "He's a good guy. Protective. You'd like him." She would. Marcus could be a little rough around the edges, but I had no doubt he curbed it in important situations or that he would charm the hell out of a guy's parents. He was definitely the kind of man good parents wanted their queer sons to bring home.

"You like this boy?"

Yes, yes I did, but that was beside the point. I didn't think anything other than sex would ever happen between us, and I didn't even know what I would *want*. Add in my upcoming move that I still needed to tell my folks about, and hookups were the extent of what I would ever have with Marcus.

"We're just friends." It might have only been recently that I felt comfortable calling him that, knowing him well enough now and all, but I did. "He's also nine years older."

"Bring him home. I want to meet him."

"Oh God, Mama. I'm not doing that. It would be weird. He's not my boyfriend."

"So? He's your friend. Friends can't meet your family? The man you're living with can't meet your family? If he's not willing to come eat some food with us, then that tells me he's up to no good."

I was fucked now. She wouldn't let this go. That wasn't how my mom worked. I loved the shit out of her, but she was as stubborn as me. "I'll talk to him." The truth was, I needed to go and see them anyway. It was past time I told them I'd be going to Atlanta soon. Telling them when Marcus was there...well, I wasn't sure how smart that was. But they'd be less likely to throw a fit that way.

"Thank you. I need to make sure he's good enough for my boy."

"Mama...it's not like that." Marcus could have any-damn-body. I highly doubted it would be me he fell for. Deciding to change the subject, I said, "Did I tell you one of my fish was sick? Luckily, they're okay now. Marcus and I went to the fish store and talked to them before we put Blue into another tank and..." Shit. That wasn't changing the subject at all.

"That's very nice of your *friend*."

"Mama..."

"That doesn't sound only friendly to me. Just sayin'."

"It would if you knew him...and now I'm going to get off the phone before you start making me think Marcus and I are secretly in love."

She laughed. "I love you, Kai."

"I know, Mama. I love you too."

We ended the call, and damn, I felt like shit. They weren't going to understand how I could want to move to Atlanta instead of returning to Riverside. But Atlanta did have a thriving queer community, and I had a really amazing opportunity there. I didn't know what the fuck I wanted to do with my life, but maybe I could end up being like Declan. He'd started out as a bartender, and now he owned Driftwood.

I fucked around Marcus's for the next couple of hours, unsure what to do. He usually got home by six unless he was meeting Corbin or one of the other Beach Bums. I got a text from Archer, giving me an update on the bar and letting me know he had a friend who could rent me an apartment. He'd sent photos, and the price was great, so I agreed immediately.

An antsy energy buzzed beneath my skin. I was bored, which yeah, I had to admit, that wasn't hard for me. I was often bored if I wasn't constantly moving. Something about that thought made me pick up my phone again and text Marcus.

Do you have plans after work?
Who is this?

I rolled my eyes. **Is that what they call an old-man joke?**

You better take that shit back, he texted, making me chuckle.

Or I could cook you dinner…if you don't have plans, that is.

It took him about ten minutes to respond. I thought he was going to ignore me, but then the text came through. **If you insist.**

If I insisted, huh? That sounded very much like someone who wanted what I'd offered but didn't want to look like he did. **I do.**

I grabbed my things, went to my car, tossed my wallet on the dashboard, and headed to the store. I wasn't sure what I wanted to make. I should have looked up some recipes before I left, but thinking things through wasn't really me.

It took a while of stalking the aisles before I made a decision. I filled the cart with everything I would need, paid, then returned to Marcus's place, windows down, the scent of the ocean filling my car.

This was definitely something I would miss in Atlanta.

Marcus had a lot of windows and tons of natural light in the house, which I fucking loved. I opened windows and turned on music, danced and sang with a side of cooking. I was really feeling The Weeknd right now, so that shit was getting extra time on my playlist.

Cooking always made me happy. I mean, people needed food, right? So there was something cool about being the one to provide it to them.

The meal was about halfway done when I spun around to the music, only to see a person standing across the kitchen from me. My heart jumped, and I thought I was about to kick some intruder's ass before I realized it was Corbin. "Shit. Sorry. I didn't hear you ring the bell." I turned the music off.

"I didn't. Sorry. I'm not used to doing that at Marcus's. I wasn't thinking."

"Oh, no. You don't have to just because I'm here. I didn't mean that."

Corbin hadn't been here a lot since I moved in. I couldn't help wondering if that was because of me. While I knew they all spent a lot of time together, I didn't know how much, so I wasn't sure if it had changed.

The oil popped in the skillet on the stove. "Fuck." I began coating my pork chops and placing them inside. "I'm making dinner for Marcus tonight. I've decided that's a thing I want to do for him. Do you want to eat with us? There's enough."

"Nah, I'm good. I don't want to interrupt. I was in the neighborhood and wanted to see what he was up to tonight."

"Then eat with us. Or if you want to hang out with him, just the two of you, that's fine. He can eat later or whatever." Corbin must be here for a reason. My dinner could wait.

"Nice dance moves," Corbin said instead of answering.

"Nice change of subject," I countered, making him laugh.

"Jesus, you're just like him. Not letting me get away with anything."

"Oh please. I'm not nearly as bad as Daddy Marcus." I winked, and Corbin chuckled.

"He's the worst."

Yeah, he was, but… "He's also kinda the best," I replied.

Corbin's forehead bunched up into a couple of wrinkles, his gaze scrutinizing me, before he said, "Yeah, he is. Are you guys gonna get married? Because I'm telling you right now, Parker isn't gonna like someone else stealing his marriage thunder until after his upcoming ceremony."

I gasped. "Gross. No. Not Marcus, of course, because he's fine as fuck, but marriage." I shuddered. "Not for me."

"No shit. Same." Corbin hopped up on the counter. "You're gonna burn your pork chops."

"Fuck." I turned to the stove and lowered the heat before flipping them. Corbin was fun, and we'd never spent time just the two of us before.

"But you like Marcus," he continued.

I shrugged because what was the point in lying? "Yeah. Who wouldn't like Marcus? We're just having fun until I leave, though."

Corbin nodded just as a sound came from the front door, and a few seconds later Marcus came into the kitchen. His gaze landed on me first, then Corbin. "Get off my counter," he said.

Corbin laughed and jumped down. "Daddy is *so* strict."

"I know, right?"

Marcus pointed at me. "Don't you start too. The two of you together means trouble." He pressed a kiss to Corbin's temple. "Hey, kid."

"Hey," Corbin replied.

"Smells good," he told me.

Corbin looked back and forth between us. "Um...so, this is cute. The two of you have become very domestic."

I pretended to gag. Marcus smacked Corbin upside the head. We were awesome, functioning adults.

"I'm making pork chops, mashed potatoes and gravy, and cornbread."

"Bone in?" Marcus cocked a brow.

"Is there any other kind?"

"That's my boy," he said, and I curtsied.

Corbin covered his mouth. "Cough—*boyfriends*—cough."

"Shut up, Corbin," Marcus and I said at the same time.

"Why is everyone always telling me to shut up?"

"Because you never do?" Marcus countered.

"You love it. Anyway, I'm outta here. Have a good night, you two crazy kids."

Marcus's gaze shot to me, and I could see the uncertainty in his stare, as if he didn't want to hurt my feelings by asking Corbin to stay, but didn't want his friend to leave either.

"Make him stay and eat with us!" I said, pulling the food from the pan and setting it on a plate. "He kept telling me no. Maybe you can force him to."

There was a silent thank-you in the private wink Marcus

sent my way. "Sit down and eat with us, Corb."

"I have shit to do."

"You'll hurt my feelings," I added.

"I'm sorry, but I'm meeting up with this guy in a little while who gives the best head I've ever had. I mean, seriously...head or pork chops? I'm sure your food is good, but I think with my dick. Ask everyone."

A snicker slipped past my lips. As far as excuses went, it was a good one.

"Jesus, don't encourage him," Marcus said playfully.

"As if I need encouragement." Corbin was backing toward the door. "I'll see you guys on Sunday, and we can swap notes about who had the best sex tonight."

"Oh my God, I love you!" I replied.

"I'd tell you to get in line, but I'd feel awful taking you away from Marcus."

"Ha-ha." Marcus was moving toward Corbin. I tried to tell him with my gaze he was fine to do whatever he had to do, and then with one more goodbye, Corbin slipped out, Marcus behind him.

I pulled the cornbread out of the oven and finished up while I waited. If Corbin needed Marcus, that was the most important thing. The food would be here afterward, and then I'd be there for whatever Marcus needed.

It was only a couple of minutes later that he came back in, though. "Is he okay?" I asked.

"Yeah, he's good. I wouldn't have let him leave otherwise. He showed me his texts. He really is meeting a hookup soon."

"Good. I didn't want him to feel like he had to leave. I know how important you two are to each other. If he needs you, that's where you should be. I'm not going anywhere... Well, I am, but not tonight."

Marcus's expression was unreadable, but then he was

stalking toward me. I moaned when he wrapped his arm around me and pulled me close. For a second I thought he was going to say something, but instead his mouth just came crashing down on mine. The kiss felt like a cross between *I want you* and *thank you*, though he didn't have anything to thank me for.

"We'll eat, and then I'll make you come." He reached down and palmed my growing erection. "How does that sound, baby boy?"

I pressed into his hand. "If I didn't know how bomb this meal is going to be, I'd say we could skip dinner and get to the orgasms."

Marcus chuckled and smacked my ass. "You should eat first. You're going to need the energy tonight."

"Best. Roommate. Ever."

We sat at the table together and had dinner, then washed the dishes before we went upstairs and Marcus made me come over and over all night.

Chapter Seventeen
Marcus

"HELLO AND WELCOME to *The Vers*, where four best friends who rarely agree on anything give their versatile opinions about everything. I'm Corbin Erickson, The Charmer."

"Marcus Alston, The Realist."

"Parker Hansley-Weaver, The Romantic."

"And I'm Declan Burns, The Loner."

It was the second Sunday since Corbin had come over when Kai had cooked dinner. I'd been slightly concerned about him that night, but after going out and talking to him, I'd felt better. Corbin wasn't good at keeping the truth from me, and if he'd been feeling some kind of way and had needed me, I would have known. Still, I'd made sure to spend more time with him over the past two weeks. Between work, hanging out with Corb, and Kai and I not only cooking dinner together every night he had off, but also breakfasts on his days off too, I'd been even more busy than usual.

For whatever reason, he insisted on making me meals. He enjoyed the kitchen, that much was clear, but I also wasn't the type of man who let people do a lot for me, which was how we'd ended up doing it together now. I couldn't imagine having any of the guys find out—especially Corbin, who would tease me, and Parker, who would think it meant more than it did.

Corbin said, "I was thinking we should have a naked game night once a week," which effectively pulled me out of my thoughts.

"Elliott and I play naked games every night." Parker pumped his eyebrows playfully.

"Stop bragging," Corbin replied, just as Declan and I said, "*No*," in unison.

Corbin pointed back and forth between the two of us. "Did you guys plan that? Before we meet up each week, do you sit down and decide how to be grumpy at the exact same time? Because I'm telling you, that's some freaky shit."

Dec said, "That would be impossible since we never know what to expect from you. How does one prepare for the hurricane that is Corbin Erickson?"

Corbin beamed. "Aww. Thank you!"

I tried to playfully smack the back of his head, but Corbin grabbed my wrist and bit my finger. "Ouch, fucker."

Parker said, "Corbin just bit Marcus. This is getting good, listeners."

"I will not be distracted from naked game night!" Corbin cut in. "We can start with Twister, and then I was thinking we could upload it to OnlyFans…you know, extra revenue and all that. Sebastian, Elliott, and Kai are welcome, of course. The more the merrier."

"How generous of you," Declan replied, but I was a little wrapped up in the fact that he'd added Kai as if he was on the same level as Elliott and Sebastian. Granted, we were talking about a fictional game of naked Twister that would never happen, but still.

Declan said, "Also, not stripping in front of my employee."

"But you would in front of the rest of us?" Parker teased.

"Corbin was right. You might have a freaky streak."

"From what I heard from Sebastian, our Dec can dirty-talk like a motherfucker." Corbin held up his hand, waiting for a high five from Declan.

"What the fuck! Bastian didn't say that." But the panicked look on Declan's face said he wasn't so sure about that.

"Whatever you say." Corbin crossed his arms, and Declan immediately swiped his cell off the table. I had no doubt he was texting Sebastian to ask.

When he set the phone down, he said, "Traitor," under his breath before blurting, "Parker has a praise kink!"

"Dec!" Parker pushed him. "Oh, wait, actually, I don't care if people know I'm Elliott's perfect boy."

I held up my hands. "This is getting a little into TMI territory. How about we get on topic now?"

"And the topic is?" Corbin asked. He had a point.

"We'll take questions before 'Mimosas and Man-Talk,'" I replied.

"I still think naked Twister would be more fun." Corbin opened up our email on the tablet. "Okay...this one is good: *How do I approach this really hot guy who is totally out of my league? I'm afraid I'm not as interesting as he is.* Aw. You're interesting. We all are in our own ways, and if he doesn't see it, then he's not worth it."

The sad thing was, Corbin believed that when it came to other people, but I doubted he did when it came to himself. He played off his low self-esteem for everyone but us.

I said, "Maybe the two of you will have things in common, but maybe you won't."

"You suck at this," Corbin told me.

"Fuck you." I laughed. "What I meant was, just because you don't have anything in common doesn't mean you're not interesting." See? I could do this. "The only way you'll ever know is if you talk to him. He's human, just like you."

"Yes," Parker said, "but sometimes really hot humans are hard to talk to for mere mortals like the rest of us. It's not always as easy to compartmentalize like you do."

I nodded. "Agreed, but that doesn't change the fact that he'll never know unless he does it."

"*Or*," Corbin said, "he could secretly stalk him, find out what he's into, and then pretend to like the same things."

"Corb!" all three of us shouted.

"I was *kidding*. Seriously, though, don't do that. I tried it once and—oops, my lawyer said I'm not supposed to talk about that," Corbin joked.

"I would like the listeners to strike that from the record," Declan teased. "You will disregard anything Corbin has ever said and will ever say in the future."

His words earned another round of laughter from all of us.

"Why is it that the three of you are always picking on me?" Corbin pouted. He was only joking, but still, I wrapped an arm around him, pulled him close, and kissed his temple. I didn't let go, and Corbin snuggled in. This...wasn't really my thing. I wasn't that touchy-feely, and usually they had to force me into the group hugs Corbin or Parker always initiated, but I also knew how much Corbin loved this shit.

"I'll read the next one." Parker reached for the tablet. Declan, who was closer, slid it over. "*Sometimes I feel like I get lost in the top/bottom/vers discussion in the queer community. I consider myself a side because I'm not into penetration. I've tried it more than once, both ways, and I find it's not for me. There are so many other things two men can do together, but a lot of guys don't consider it sex unless one person ends up with their dick in someone's ass.* It's signed: Sides Need Love Too."

Corbin said, "There are a whole lot of ways to have sex—

sucking, frotting, jerking off. I hook up with this guy who is a side, and we still make each other come our brains out."

I added, "Anal penetration is great for those who are into it, but it's extremely heteronormative to pretend that's the only way to have sex."

"And boring," Parker chimed in. "Being creative with sex is half the fun."

"Good boy." Corbin winked at him, making Parker flip him off.

Declan said, "I think the most important part is not shaming anyone for what they want—penetration or not. Sex is so incredibly personal, and we should all be fucking the way that works for us. If someone can't respect your sexual desires, then they don't deserve to be with you. I think there are likely more sides out there than people realize." Declan ran a hand through his hair.

"Which is part of the problem," I said. "People are afraid of being shamed."

"Sex and dating are complicated as fuck," Parker said. "But conversations like this help."

We all agreed, then answered a few more questions before going into "Mimosas and Man-Talk," where we talked about current events, recent movies, and things like that. I ended the show by sharing the prompts I had from our sponsors, and then we stopped recording.

"I think Marcus and Kai are boyfriends!" Corbin blurted out.

"What the fuck, Corb?" I grumbled.

"Did I tell you guys that Kai asked me for sex advice about Marcus?" Declan said.

"Wow…that bad in the sack, are you?" Corbin asked me.

Like I so often did, I pretended not to hear him. "We're not boyfriends. We're hooking up while he lives here. He's moving to Atlanta." Which he still needed to tell his parents about. It was strange to me, how nervous he was about it. I couldn't imagine the kind of reaction he was expecting because my parents would be proud of me if I was doing something to further my career that way. We were so different in that.

It took me a moment to realize none of them had replied, but they were all looking at me like cartoon characters with their mouths open and their eyes bugged out.

Parker collected himself first. "So are you saying the fact that he's moving is the only reason you're not boyfriends? If it wasn't for that, you would want to be?"

"What? No!" How in the hell had they gotten that from my response?

"Because the Marcus I know would have just said you're not boyfriends and you don't want to be. Instead, you qualified it with Kai moving."

Oh fuck. He was right. I had. What the hell had that been about? "That's not what I meant." I stood and left the room. Like I knew they would, all three of them followed.

The house was empty besides us. Elliott was with his friend Vaughn, Kai had picked up an extra shift at Driftwood, and Sebastian was doing whatever it was movie stars did when they wrote their own screenplay and would be meeting with some execs soon to see what they could do with it.

"What *did* you mean?" Declan asked.

"Oh Jesus. Not you too. I meant he's not my boyfriend. What else was I supposed to mean?" This kind of situation was a whole lot easier when I was on the other side of it.

"They're so cute and domestic," Corb said. "I came over one night, and Kai was cooking him dinner."

"Nice, Corb. And I planned to hang out with you after this. Not anymore."

"You still will because you love me and I can make you do anything. It's part of my charm."

Damn him for being right.

"Kai likes cooking." I opened the fridge to see what we should have for lunch.

"And apparently you like him," Parker teased.

I turned to Declan. "Control your best friend."

He smirked. "The way you control Corbin?"

Who responded by singing, "*Marcus loves Kai.*" Fuck my life. Sometimes having friends was the worst. Then, "Do you think Kai will care if I call him Daddy too? It is Marcus's nickname, after all, so it makes sense that I would need to call his boyfriend the same."

Knowing exactly what I was going to do, Corbin started running a split second before I gave chase. He sped out the back door toward the beach, with me right behind him. I tackled him, both of us falling fully clothed into the surf. Seconds later Declan and Parker were there too, and while their teasing drove me up the wall, in my head I could admit that having friends wasn't the worst—it was actually the best.

And I'd rather think about that than my complicated feelings about Kai…

Chapter Eighteen
Kai

"WHAT CAN I get you, ba—gorgeous," I asked a guy sitting with his friends at a table in Driftwood. My head cocked slightly at the fact that I'd changed what I was going to call him. *Baby* was fun and flirty. I used it with a lot of men, but I also used it with Marcus, and now...well, shit. Now randos couldn't be *baby* because Marcus was. I didn't even call him Teddy anymore. This development made my stomach flip uncomfortably but also piqued my interest. I'd never cared about something like that before.

"What about you? Are you on the menu?" the guy asked, and I had to admit, he was really hot. He was Asian, with black hair that went down to his shoulders. He dressed nice, in a button-up shirt, and was similar in size to me.

Normally, he'd be one hundred percent someone I would hook up with, but then I thought about Marcus and whatever it was we were doing. We'd agreed to fuck around until I moved to Atlanta, though we hadn't talked about exclusivity. Still, while this sexy flirt would definitely be a good time, I realized I didn't want anyone else right now. Marcus kept me plenty satisfied. I just wanted to enjoy this time, enjoy him, and then be on my way.

The hard part was, I *did* like to flirt—without leading the other person on, so I winked and said, "Not available. You can look but don't touch."

"Fuuuuck," he responded with a good-natured smile. "You would have been fun."

"Yes, I would have. Now, what can I get you to drink?"

He ordered, and then I took his friends' requests too. He gave me his credit card, asked for a tab, and I went back to the bar. I stumbled, almost tripping when I looked up and saw Marcus there. He was at the end of the counter, nursing a drink and looking fine as always. Heat pooled in my gut, then shot up my spine, telling me yes, I'd been right. There was no one other than Marcus I wanted right now.

"Fancy seeing you here," I said, making my way behind the counter. "Did you come to see me?"

"Nah, just wanted a drink."

"Aw, you missed me. Don't worry. I missed you too, baby." I began mixing the alcohol.

"Who's the guy?" Marcus motioned behind him, where my flirt was.

"Why? Jealous?"

"I don't get jealous."

Yeah, right. Maybe not in the I-love-you way, but Marcus wasn't one to share. "Now my feelings are hurt. I wanted you to tell me no one else can have me. That while I'm here, I'm yours." I leaned over the counter. He had his elbow resting on it, glass in his hand. "But even though you don't care if I took him in the bathroom, I told him he can look but not touch." Then I licked his finger before biting it, making Marcus almost drop his glass. He fisted it, pinning me with a dark stare filled with lust.

"You're playing with fire," he warned.

"You told me that before, but I have yet to get burned… Could be fun, no?" I smiled, grabbed the drinks, and walked away. One quick glance over my shoulder showed that Marcus had turned on his stool and was watching. I gave an extra shake to my hips as I went.

"Looks like I'm not the only one watching," the flirt said as soon as I handed him a glass. "He the reason you can't play?"

It was on the tip of my tongue to say no. I wasn't really the kind of guy to get told what I could do that way, to get put on lockdown without it at least being something we discussed, but still I said, "Yeah."

"He gonna kick my ass?"

"Not as long as you're good."

Once I was finished there, I continued to the next group. I didn't have to turn to feel Marcus's intense stare. People flirted with me, and I flirted back because that was just what you did in a career like this—at least when you were single, and though Marcus and I were fucking, I wasn't silly enough to think we were in a relationship.

It wasn't until I was on my way back to the bar that I remembered Declan wasn't working tonight, so...Marcus really had come here to see me. My heart did a strange flip-flop that raised a couple of red flags, which I promptly ignored.

"Half the men in this bar right now want you," Marcus said when I approached.

"Only half?" I frowned, and he chuckled.

I started toward the bar so I could make more drinks, but he grabbed my wrist, holding me in place. It wasn't tight. If I wanted free, all I had to do was pull back, but this was Marcus, so I definitely didn't want out of his hold.

"It's hot knowing they want you but can't have you." He brushed his thumb over the throbbing pulse in my wrist. My breathing picked up. Somehow he'd changed the tables on me really fucking quickly. When I'd bit him earlier, I'd had the upper hand, but it belonged to Marcus now, and he pressed his advantage. "That you want my dick so bad, you'll tell all these other fools you're taken because you're mine until you go."

If we weren't in a busy bar and I wasn't at work, there was no doubt in my mind that I would've dropped to my knees right then. But I was also an ornery little shit, so I said, "Only if that means you belong to me too until I leave." Wow. That had come out much more confident than I felt at the moment.

"Yeah, but I don't have a trail of admirers everywhere I go."

Holy shit. I hadn't expected him to agree to it, but then it wasn't as if we were making promises, just agreeing to exclusively sleep with each other until I moved across the country. "Have you seen you? Everyone wants you."

Marcus shrugged like he didn't care, then pulled me between his legs, and I let him. He ran his hands up and down my back, admitting, "I like having something they want."

That was...surprising, but also not, and very, *very* hot. "You like it when I flirt or people flirt with me but know they can't have me?"

"At least for tonight. It's been a strange day."

"What's wrong?" My concern for him overpowered how hot what he'd said was.

"Nothing. You should kiss me and then go back to work. People are waiting on their drinks."

Oh shit. He was right. I'd somehow forgotten I actually had a job to do. Luckily, we were pretty well staffed tonight. I leaned forward and pressed my mouth to his. Marcus snaked his tongue past my lips and held the back of my head, deepening the kiss. I hadn't expected him to be so thorough in public, but then, this was about his possessive streak that maybe shouldn't have been so sexy but was. I liked being Marcus's and him being mine—well, I liked us pretending that was the case.

When he pulled back, my cock throbbed, and I groaned. "So not fair. You got me going, and I can't do anything about it."

"Are you complaining?"

"Shut up," I replied because goddamn it, I wasn't.

I sneaked behind the bar, apologized to Eliza, and started making drinks.

Marcus's stare rarely left me all night. He watched everything I did. I laughed at things men said, flirted playfully but made sure they all knew I wasn't going home with any of them.

When one man put a hand on my shoulder, I gently removed it and pointed to Marcus, who raised his drink. "He's mine," I said.

"Are you sure you don't mean you're his?"

"That too." I winked.

Suddenly it felt like we were both playing with fire, both teasing the edge of something dangerous because I wasn't Marcus's and he wasn't mine. We were just fucking, and I was leaving, and even if I weren't, we were totally different.

So I kissed my fingers and pressed them to the customer's cheek before walking away. Marcus's gaze turned darker—not angry, but like he was really fucking turned on. It held me, wrapped me up as I got closer and closer to him.

The bar had slowed down some, and it was time for my break, so I didn't stop until I reached him. When I did, I grabbed his hand and pulled him to his feet.

"I'm gonna take my break real quick," I told Eliza, who chuckled.

"Is that what we're calling it nowadays?" she ribbed as I

led Marcus behind the counter.

"Naughty girl. I have no idea what you're talking about," I joked back.

I unlocked the door to the back and went down the same hallway I had with Marcus the night he'd asked me to move in with him. The second the door to Declan's office was closed behind us, I said, "You should probably remind me now that I'm yours."

"Jesus, what is it about you?" Marcus asked before his mouth crushed mine. The kiss was frantic, like this was a one-off and we had to take everything we could in that moment. His tongue pushed between my lips, and then he retreated so I could taste him too.

I went to open his pants, but he swatted my hands away, then sank to his knees.

"Fuck yes." My dick was really fucking hard, and the thought of being in Marcus's mouth almost made me blow my load right then.

He quickly worked open my pants, then shoved them and my underwear down. My erection pointed at him, a pearl of precum at the tip. Marcus spit in his hand, then slowly stroked my shaft. "Who do you want?"

"You...fuck...just you." Maybe I shouldn't have added the *just*. That made it sound more real, but Marcus didn't call me on it, and I didn't want to focus on it.

His mouth wrapped around me, and he immediately sucked me to the back of his throat.

"Holy shit." My eyes fell closed as he bobbed on my cock, lips lowering enough to touch my nuts. I wasn't a small guy, but Marcus could deep throat a fucking dick.

My skin had to taste like sweat, my body musky and masculine, but he didn't seem to care, and I knew if the situation were reversed, I'd be the same. I loved those very things when I was with a man.

My balls were high and tight, just waiting to unleash in Marcus's mouth. He reached around and grabbed my ass, pulling me tighter against him, urging me on, so I began to fuck his face.

"So good, baby," I said, my hand on his head. "Been wanting this all night. Not any of them. You make me feel like I can fucking fly." Words fell out of my mouth, and I thought that maybe I would die right then and there, my dick in the wet suction of Marcus's mouth.

When his finger teased my crease before sneaking down between my legs to rub my taint, I gave in. My orgasm made me splinter apart from the inside out, my body jittery with a huge buildup, and then released in spurt after spurt, all of which Marcus swallowed down.

The second I finished, it was like my body wanted to give out. I nearly collapsed, but he shoved to his feet, opened his pants, and tugged them and his underwear down.

"I'll suck you off," I said, but he stopped me.

"Lift your shirt."

I did as Marcus said. He spit on his hand again, this time using it to stroke his own dick. His arm moved quickly, tugging at his long, thick erection. He was so beautiful, so sexy and strong. I swear sometimes he looked like a fucking king.

Marcus growled, his muscles tightening as his cum shot from his cock, the first splash landing on my groin, then my cock and my stomach. He came all over me. When his balls were milked dry, Marcus rubbed his load into my skin. "Now you'll smell like me the rest of the night, and they'll know you're mine."

Holy.

Shit.

"I think that might be the hottest thing I've ever heard."

Marcus pulled up my underwear, then my jeans, buttoning and zipping them for me before he did the same for himself. "See you at home, baby boy."

He made it all the way to the door before I asked, "Are you okay? Did something happen?"

"It doesn't matter." He kept his back to me.

"It does to me." *He* mattered to me.

Marcus sighed. "My parents canceled dinner. It's nothing new. I don't know why I let it bother me. I'm too old for that shit."

"No one is ever too old to need to feel loved or important to people they care about." I walked over to him, wrapped my arms around his waist from behind, and kissed his nape.

"I have the Beach Bums for that."

But he hadn't gone to see any of them tonight. He'd come here…to me. What was going on? "You're important to me, Marcus."

He didn't respond right away. "I want you in my bed when you come home tonight."

"Okay."

And then, without another word, he walked out.

Chapter Nineteen
Marcus

A COUPLE OF days later, I was still trying to figure out that possessive shit I'd pulled on Kai. The weird dichotomy of watching him flirt and knowing he wouldn't let other men have him while we were fucking was…hell, how did I explain it? It made fire ignite in my gut, lick up my spine, and basically completely consume me.

That I could explain away easier than telling him I wanted him in my bed. And that he'd been there each night since. Easy sex? Yes. He was right next to me, so I could pull him close and touch him anytime I wanted. I wasn't a stupid man, though. I also wasn't a liar and couldn't let myself pretend there wasn't something else twisted up with how much I wanted him physically.

I liked Kai, and I had no idea what the fuck to do about it—or what I wanted to do about it. I'd never experienced anything like this before, and I had to admit, it was inconvenient that I was now, with someone nine years younger, who wanted independence and planned to move across the country.

And that just covered some of the logistics…logistics I had no goddamned reason to even be thinking about because, again, I didn't know what this meant or what I wanted, and I sure as shit didn't think I'd be any good at it. I wasn't made for something like what Declan and Sebastian had, or Parker and Elliott. I couldn't say the words they did and didn't know how to be who a partner needed me to be.

These thoughts had been plaguing me for days, and I was really fucking done with it. I wasn't one to get all up in my head like this. I preferred facts over emotions because they were a whole lot easier to deal with.

I had a feeling some of this was coming from the conversation with the Beach Bums about liking Kai, as well as from currently being on my way to my folks' house for lunch. For once they didn't cancel, and there I was, clearing my afternoon to meet with them.

They'd designed their own home, which was different from the one I grew up in. It was sleek and modern, with hard lines. Like my place, it was bigger than what they needed, the two of them able to get lost enough that they could be home together and not run into each other unless they wanted to.

They'd never said it, but I was pretty sure they hadn't wanted kids, that I hadn't been planned. They'd been older when I was born and hadn't slowed down in the least.

I parked in the driveway and headed to the large, black front door set against the white house. I rang the bell, and a few seconds later, my dad was inviting me in. He wore slacks and a white button-up even though he wasn't working. Gray curls were peppered throughout the black ones, his hair always freshly done.

"Hey, son. Good to see you."

"You too, Dad." We shook hands, which I knew was different from most people, but that was just who we'd always been. I wouldn't know what to do if my dad suddenly hugged me.

"Sorry it's been so crazy. Your mother wants to open a San Francisco office, and we've been traveling back and

THE REALIST

forth."

Well, shit. That was news to me. They were seventy years old, but it didn't surprise me that they were still taking on even more responsibility.

"Why?" I asked, following him through the living room.

"You know how she is."

I knew how they both were. They liked to put the blame on each other, but they were the exact same: work, work, work.

Like you?

I shook that thought from my head. "Where is Mom?"

He went outside, and I followed. When home, they spent a lot of time in their backyard, the way I did too. The weather was almost always perfect in Santa Monica, so why not?

"She's finishing up at the salon, then grabbing our lunch."

We sat in chairs at one of the tables outside. The yard was perfectly manicured and had a pool and a kitchen, same as mine.

"How's work going?" Dad asked.

We talked business because that's mostly what we had in common. What they had would belong to me one day, and I had no clue what the fuck I would even want to do with it. I'd have to keep it, but now I was thinking that if we had a San Francisco office as well, that was just more on my plate. It was selfish because I was lucky as shit, but that was how I felt.

It wasn't too long until Mom got home, carrying two bags of food. Dad immediately got up to take them from her. They did things like that often, helped in those small ways. To some, he treated her like a queen, the way she deserved, but it was with a detachment you didn't see in people in love with each other.

"Hey, baby," she said, sitting beside me. "You're letting your hair go. You need to clean up this fade." She touched my scalp, and I pulled my head away.

"I know."

"You need to look professional at work. If you don't, no one will take you seriously."

"I'm one of the highest-ranked agents in Los Angeles County. I think I'll be okay."

"I was just trying to help," she replied, and I sighed.

"I know. What's new?"

Dad was pulling out food as we went on to discuss work and the business yet again, now from Mom's point of view.

She'd gotten Italian from one of their favorite places. I tried to change the subject to the food and how good my ravioli was, but they kept getting back on the topic of my company or Alston Architecture.

Eventually, I said, "Parker and Elliott are getting married at my place this coming summer."

"Which one is Parker?" Mom asked.

Dad said, "He's Marcus's best friend. The one who was bigger as a kid."

"No, Dad, that's Corbin. Parker is the baker." They've been my friends since middle school, and yet my folks still couldn't remember which one was which… "Never mind. I have a friend staying with me right now. Kai."

"Boyfriend?" Mom asked. They had never given a shit that I was gay. That was one thing I'd never worried about. Like most things about me, it was just a fact to them and didn't require much feeling.

"If this is serious," Dad said, "and you plan on marrying this man, you need to start considering a prenup. Have you spoken to Lawrence?"

"No. Hell no. I didn't talk to our attorney about Kai. Jesus, I never even said we were together, and you already have him trying to steal my money. You don't know him."

Mom said, "It's not personal, Marcus, but we've worked really damn hard to have what we do. Is it so wrong to want to protect it?" And I did get what she meant. Every single thing they had accomplished had been with hard work and grit. They hadn't been handed anything the way I had been. They had to work much harder to have the things they did, and that meant something to them, but their assumptions about Kai made my skin feel too tight.

"He's a friend. And he's moving to Atlanta soon." Though we still didn't have an exact date, which didn't sit well with me. "He needed a place to stay, and I'm helping him out, is all." And now I was pissed at myself. Kai was more than just someone I was helping out. Fuck, why had I brought him up in the first place?

Mom scrutinized me. "Something is different in your voice."

"No, it's not."

She nodded, but I wasn't sure she believed me. We got off the conversation about Kai, though. We ate and talked. Once the food was gone, Mom took the plates inside, and they told me about a new client and some issues they'd had with one of their designs.

The whole time, I found myself watching them in a new way. They didn't shoot small smiles at each other the way Declan and Sebastian did. They didn't touch the way Parker and Elliott did. It wasn't because they were older and had spent their whole lives together—I couldn't ever remember them doing that. They weren't affectionate with each other. When you looked at them, they were business partners who lived together.

They both had their cells close, checking messages often. When Dad's rang, he said, "I need to take this," and disappeared inside. Mom watched him go, and I knew it was because she itched to get back to work. They both always did, and while I respected the hell out of them for it, sometimes it felt pretty fucking empty.

"I hope nothing is wrong," she said.

"If it is, you guys will figure it out."

"I still wish you worked with us. I understand wanting to make your own way, but Alston Architecture is our legacy, Marcus, and it'll be yours one day."

"I know. I won't let you down." And I wouldn't, but I also didn't want to talk about it. "Are you in love with Dad?" fell out of my mouth before I could stop myself.

"What on earth? Why would you ask that?"

It wasn't a yes. It wasn't a no either, but if I were to ask Parker the same about Elliott, his first response would be yes, and then he would ask why. "Who knows? Ignore me."

Mom sighed. "Your father and I fit well together, Marcus. We always have. Maybe we don't show it the way others do, but we don't need to."

But what if *I*'d needed it as a kid? To have them cuddle on the couch and for me to go and sit with them while we watched movies and talked about our day. Not that they could change who they were for me, but that was all I knew now, and for most people, it wasn't enough.

Corbin, Declan, and Parker accepted me the way I was, and I trusted them enough to let them pull me into their ridiculous hugs. I could hold Corbin when he needed it because they had shown me what love *looked* like in physical form, not just the words. And I'd only ever had that with them.

"Where is this coming from? Is this about Kai?"

I shook my head. Maybe it was about him to some degree, but it was also about me. "Nah, I'm good. I don't know why I asked that."

Her brows drew together, and there was real concern there. "You know we love you, right, Marcus?"

I nodded because I did, but knowing and feeling or seeing weren't the same thing.

Chapter Twenty

Kai

I HAD A feeling Marcus was going to be down when he got home this evening, so I wanted to treat him to something special. I'd been racking my brain, trying to think of something Marcus would like, when I remembered a random conversation between him and Corbin. They were talking about astronomy and how Marcus was really interested in galaxies and planets and stargazing, which had surprised me. Maybe because Marcus was so grounded in day-to-day facts, I supposed, and at first glance, astronomy didn't seem like something he'd enjoy. But then, it was science. If I thought about it, it made sense he'd find it appealing.

So I'd made a trip to the store earlier, spending money I didn't really have, and then got everything prepared. He'd messaged to say he would be working after he was done with his folks and would be home around six like always. As hard as it was, I didn't mention that it was cute as hell when he did things like that. How did he not realize how he was always thinking about others? That he was always so considerate? He had more heart than he would ever be willing to acknowledge.

As I waited for Marcus to get home, my stomach flopped around in a stupid, annoying way, though I had absolutely no reason to be nervous. Also, I didn't do nervous when it came to men. I had fun with them, just the way Marcus and I were

THE REALIST

doing.

Still, when I heard the door open, I felt like I was going to throw up. But then Marcus walked into the room, and my knees went a little weak. All I could do was remember him shooting his load all over me the other day and rubbing it in so I smelled like him. Talk about hot as fuck.

"You don't have to keep cooking for me," he said.

"I didn't cook for you. Just me. I already ate."

"Oh shit. I didn't—you're lying."

I smiled. "Yeah, I am. But you're not allowed to complain because I did this really super sweet thing for you, and if you do complain, it'll hurt my feelings." I walked over to him, put a hand on his chest, and smelled fresh soap on his skin. "You don't want to hurt my feelings, do you, baby?"

"You really like causing trouble, don't you?" He swatted my ass playfully. "One of these days you're gonna get yourself into a situation with me you can't get out of."

On the surface, it didn't look like anything was wrong, but my gut told me there was, and that he would hide it and pretend he was okay because that's what he did. He was the rock for everyone around him and never let them know he needed things too.

"Maybe I won't want to get out of it." I shrugged, leaned in, and nipped his lip. "You smell good."

"I went to the gym for a little while. Showered there."

"Damn it. I love the smell of sweat on a man's skin too."

He growled and reached for me, but I twisted free before he could get ahold. "Stop being bad. You'll distract me."

"I'm the bad one? That's you. And don't play like you don't want me to find all sorts of creative ways to distract you."

He reached for me again, trying to wrap his arms around my waist. I swatted his hands away. "Daddy's in a mood tonight, isn't he?"

"Saying that to me sure as shit isn't going to help my current situation." He grabbed his crotch, showing me his very obvious erection behind his shorts.

It was my turn to groan. "Not gonna lie, I'm trying not to drool, but dinner first, sex later. Let's go upstairs." I'd prepared everything on the balcony.

Marcus followed me to his room, and when I opened the glass doors, I knew without looking that he froze in place. I felt the confusion radiating off him, the heaviness in the air as he wrestled with whether to allow himself to appreciate this.

The first thing he said was, "Wait, I thought you worked tonight."

"I got someone to cover my shift." And he'd still texted to say when he was getting home even though he didn't think I'd be here? Fuck, this man. He made me feel all jittery inside. "But I also hung these lights, I hope you don't mind. I thought they would enhance the mood."

Everything we needed was there—a small fridge, his outdoor futon stacked with pillows, a gas firepit, his hot tub. I'd added the lighting because it was cute, then brought out the food and drinks and—

"A telescope?"

"It's not a really good one. You might have a better one. I didn't want to ask and ruin the surprise, so...*surprise!*" I threw my arms in the air, hoping I looked extra cute.

"How did you..."

"You mentioned it to Corbin one time."

He ran his fingers over the telescope, which was perched on a tripod.

"I'm very, very good at spoiling people. I even made a jazz and blues playlist because you're old and I think you like that stuff."

He laughed, rich and deep, the sound working its way inside me and soothing my nerves. Then his expression sobered, his dark brows pulling together. "Come here."

We were standing about five feet away from each other, but I didn't budge. "What if I don't want to?" I was a fucking boss for not jumping into his arms and telling him to take me now, even as we both knew it was exactly what I wanted.

"Come here," he said again, his voice lower, raspier, and, well, this was one of those moments I really wanted Marcus to tell me what to do and to obey, so I went.

"Yes?"

This time when he wrapped his arms around me, I let him. Marcus held me tight, forehead pressed to mine, his eyes closed. "Thank you."

My heart got way too mushy for comfort, like Marcus was doing things to it that I had never experienced before, making it want to open up and not only let him in, but maybe tackle him and drag him there even if he didn't want to go. "Nothing to thank me for, baby. Now let's eat before it gets cold."

I'd gotten one of those bags delivery drivers used to keep the food warm, and grabbed the containers from inside.

"I smoked the ribs. I made my own seasoning too, wanted to try something different. It'll have a little kick to it, almost like a Cajun flavor. I hope that's okay."

"Sounds damn good to me. I love ribs."

"I know." I grinned as we set the containers on the small table. I wasn't going to pretend I wasn't proud of myself for paying attention…or not being afraid to ask questions.

Marcus chuckled. "You're a cheater. Who did you ask?"

"I'm not telling my secrets."

"Corbin."

"Corbin who?"

We sat at the table together. I'd made the ribs and green beans with bacon, onion, and garlic—as if there was any other way to have them—and homemade mac and cheese, all of which were favorites of his when he allowed himself to eat unhealthily. As we ate, I had to force myself not to ask him how it went with his folks. It was killing me not to know, but it also wasn't my business, and I wanted Marcus to have a good night. He deserved to have a good night, one where he felt how special he was.

"I heard you gave Corbin his first kiss when you guys were teenagers." I was fascinated by their stories because I never had that. Archer and I were chill, and he was doing me a solid with this job, but we didn't have the kind of relationship the Beach Bums had. I wasn't sure many people in the world did.

"Yep."

I waited a moment for him to elaborate, and when he didn't, I prompted, "And?"

"And what? We kissed. The end."

I rolled my eyes. "Why? How did that come about? I don't know. Just making conversation, Mr. One-Word Answers."

He pointed a rib at me. "Be nice. This is my day, right?"

It was, and I was surprised he'd acknowledged what I was doing. "Ugh. I guess. Please tell me your stories, Marcus. I want to know everything about you."

His nose wrinkled up, and I had to admit, that likely wasn't something I should have said, but it was true. Marcus sighed. "I've told you some about him already, and at the time, he was having a down day, feeling low about himself. Some kids had played a prank on him. He was talking to someone online, kinda like how we'd met, only it was people from his school. Corb thought it was a boy like him—queer and insecure. He'd kept it from me. I think he knew I would go all…well, *me* about it. I would have doubted this kid was who he said he was, and Corbin needed him to be what he wanted. It's not always easy to deal with someone who tells it like it is."

"No, but you never do it in a hurtful way, and it always comes from the heart." It was only because Marcus loved his friends so much. And also, I thought his realism was a way of protecting himself and those he cared about.

"That doesn't mean it can't hurt. So…he goes to meet with this punk, thinking he's going to get his first kiss. Only it was a group of assholes from school, and they made fun of him for it. He came to see me afterward, and…I just wanted to help. I told him the truth, that he was beautiful and that I loved him. When he stopped crying and felt better, he said he would rather his first kiss be with someone he loved too and asked if I would do it, so I did."

That was…fuck, I didn't even know how to describe that. "I think that's the most beautiful thing I've ever heard."

Marcus rolled his eyes. "He chose me because he knew exactly what it would be with me. Yes, I loved him, but it didn't mean anything beyond that. It was simply giving a friend something he needed."

"He chose you because you're his best friend and you're a good man, and he knew it would be truly special if it was with you." It didn't surprise me when Marcus shrugged off my comment. "You do a lot for them."

"They do a lot for me. I don't think…" He shook his head. "I don't think I ever felt like my existence was important or like I was needed until I had them. I hadn't experienced what love *felt* like, if that makes sense. It was this thing I knew I had. The way I was provided for, the things I was given, the way my folks wanted what was best for me. Those things are love, but they don't feel like the heart of it. Like, it's always at a distance rather than up close and personal the way it is with the Beach Bums. My folks can give me shit, they can give me fucking everything, but I can't do the same for them. What do they need from me? Not affection and attention the way Corbin does. They don't need me the way Declan did when his parents would take off or treat him like shit. They don't need to be reassured the way Park does. Fuck. Ignore me. I can't believe I said all that."

For a moment, all I could do was watch him. What did you say to something like that? It was deep and honest and both beautiful and heartbreaking at the same time. Corbin, Parker, and Declan were so lucky to be loved by Marcus and to have the privilege to love him in return.

Chapter Twenty-One
Marcus

I COULDN'T READ the expression on Kai's face, and I'd never wanted to take my words back as much as I did right then. What the fuck kind of pull did he have on me? How did he get this shit out of me without even trying? Why did he make me want to give him more?

I was too fucking raw today, and that wasn't something I allowed myself to feel very often. Usually I was good at compartmentalizing that, putting it away into little boxes in the back of my head. Even with the Beach Bums, I was able to do that because it was easier to be there for them. And I loved being there for them rather than letting them in on my shit, but for whatever reason, with Kai I couldn't stop.

"I like you," he said, surprising me. He'd said it before, but it sounded different now.

"Excuse me?" Maybe not the best thing to say, but it was what came out.

"I like you, and I don't totally know what I mean by that, so I don't want you to freak out and run. I know what this is—sex and friendship. And I'm planning on moving soon, but I also don't want to lie to you. I like you in a way I've never liked someone I was fucking before. That's all I know for now."

I wasn't often left speechless, but Kai had done it, and in

fact, every time I did feel this way, it was because of him.

I waited for the urge to hit me to do exactly what he'd said and run. Well, not run because I didn't really work that way, but to tell him there was no point in liking me and to remind him we were just fucking, but neither of those things happened. I almost didn't believe my own voice when I said, "I like you too…but I haven't sorted through how I feel about that."

"You and me both. I mean…fucking hell, yeah, because you're Marcus and you're fine and have a big heart, but I'm twenty-six and don't even know what the hell I'm doing with my life, so falling for a man isn't smart."

"Yeah, well, I'm thirty-five, and I don't think it's smart for me either."

"At least we're on the same page."

"There's that, but also…I wouldn't know the first thing about being in a relationship. They're not easy. While I'm a workaholic in other ways, I'm not sure I'm cut out for that kind of pressure."

"Do you believe that?"

"Which part?"

"That you don't know the first thing about being in one. Jesus, Marcus. For someone who tells others to be real and who usually is in other areas of his life, you don't see yourself clearly at all. I'm not sure I've ever met someone who would be better in a relationship than you…who loves the way you do." I almost swallowed my tongue before he added, "I'm not saying you love me. I meant your friends. Let yourself see how incredible you are."

"I see myself just fine." I shifted uncomfortably.

"Liar, liar, pants on fire. But we'll deal with that another time. The food's getting cold. I have one more question. What do we do? Just keep on keeping on while knowing we like each other, but because of life, it likely won't go anywhere?"

I shrugged. The only other answer was to stop spending time with him, and I sure as shit wasn't doing that. For the first time since my three best friends, I looked forward to spending time with someone who I knew felt the same for me. "I can't think of a better answer. As long as we're honest and we're both realistic about what this is."

Kai laughed. "Oh, Daddy, you and your damn realism."

"Stop being ornery," I said, chuckling too.

"So...you've liked me for a long time, huh? That's why you took me up to your room to mess around?"

Well, this was going too far. "I thought you only had one more question and you were gonna stop being ornery?" When he shrugged, I said, "I'm not answering that shit." But on some level he was right, and I knew my not answering told him that.

"Mm-hm," Kai replied flirtatiously. "I'll let it go for now."

We ate together and stopped talking about feelings and liking each other and all that stuff that made me uncomfortable. Kai could cook like no one's business, and I made sure to tell him that more than once. When we were done, we stripped out of our clothes and got into the hot tub. It was getting dark, stars beginning to make an appearance.

Kai said, "Can I ask you something?"

"Nope," I teased.

"Ha-ha. Seriously, though...and this has nothing to do with me liking you in *that way*, but...I need to go see my family, and my mama is curious about this sugar daddy I told her I'm living with."

"Kai..."

"So I was thinking..."

I was going to kill him. "Kai, you'd better not have told

your family that."

He laughed. "No, I didn't. I told her we're friends. But she's curious about you because I'm her baby and she loves me, so she wants to make sure you're not an asshole. So I was wondering if you would be willing to come with me to see them this weekend. We won't tell them we're fucking."

"I should hope not, but knowing you…"

"Jerk." He blew me a kiss. "Meet my family. You're important to me, so you'll be important to them. I want you to have that."

My fucking heart nearly exploded. He was going to kill me because the things that were going on inside me when he said that… Fuck, I didn't know how to accept them. How I would deal with it when he took them away.

But I also knew Kai needed this, not just because he wanted me to be around his family, but because he had to tell them about Atlanta, and I would have his back if I was there.

"It's not a thing, Marcus. I don't think it means something it doesn't or—"

"Yes," I said simply.

"Excuse me? *Yes?*"

"Don't make a big deal about it."

He shoved to his feet, naked, his cock soft and hanging between his legs, and he punched his hands in the air like he was cheering. "He said yes!" Kai shouted.

"Oh God. Get the fuck out of here with that shit. It sounds like you proposed."

"Shit. No. Ew," he replied. I grinned, my chest weirdly fluttery and light when I grabbed him and pulled him to my lap. Kai straddled me, resting his arms on my shoulders. "Thank you for liking me…for not thinking I'm too much."

Maybe that was what I needed—someone other people thought of that way. Corbin was my best friend, and he'd heard similar things, but when I looked at Corb, I didn't feel the things that twisted up my chest when I looked at Kai. "Fuck any-damn-body who makes you feel like you're too much. I like the way you are."

I slid my hands up and down his back, one grabbing his ass, the other holding the back of his head, his mouth close to mine. Kai tried to kiss me, but I didn't let him. "Patience, baby boy." My cock was throbbing, and his was now pointing out of the water, having grown stiff too. "You gonna be good for me tonight? Listen to everything I say? Because that's the only way to get what you want."

"Emotions made you feel out of control, so you need to get that back?" he asked against my mouth, and damn him for being right.

"This would be a whole lot easier if you didn't call me on my shit."

Kai smiled. "But then I wouldn't be me." He tried to kiss me again, but I didn't let him. "God, you jerk. Yes. I'll be good and do what you want."

"Then you can kiss me."

"Thank fuck." Kai lashed his tongue against my lips, then swept it inside. I let him lead for a moment before I took over, pushing mine into his mouth while pulling his body closer against me.

My finger teased his crack, working closer and closer to his hole. When Kai whimpered against my lips, I pulled back. When he leaned in for another kiss, I shook my head. "That was just a taste. I know you're hungry for it, but you're gonna have to wait."

"Argh! Fuck you!" Kai said, pouting.

"Someone went through all the trouble to get me a telescope, so I want to look at the stars with them."

"Oh…"

I quirked a brow at him. "Yeah, now you're okay with it. Up."

"Yep. You're definitely in Bossy Marcus mode."

"Baby boy, even when I don't show it, I'm in Bossy Marcus mode."

"So fucking hot." Kai smirked and climbed off me. We grabbed towels, dried off, and I got us each a robe. Kai's was new, but I didn't tell him that, didn't say I'd bought it in case he was ever in my room and used the hot tub.

"I was better at this when I was a kid. Let's see if I can still find the constellations."

"Aww, you were a nerd."

"I was a badass motherfucker and still am."

"I know you are, baby." He patted my arm as if placating me.

"I'm not playin'."

Kai laughed. "Wow. You're taking this very seriously. You were a badass motherfucker. I know."

I grinned because goddamn, he could make me do that like no one else could.

He'd said the telescope wasn't expensive, but still I worried about the cost. Kai was planning a move, and I knew money was tight for him. As much as I wanted to, I didn't let myself ask if I could reimburse him. I didn't want to insult him or look like I didn't appreciate what he'd done for me because I did, more than I could ever express. This night meant something to me in a way nothing ever had before.

It was blurry when I looked through the eyepiece. I worked on adjusting it until the white spots dancing against the midnight sky were clear and sharp.

"Is it working okay?" Kai asked.

"Yeah, you wanna see? Then I'll look for constellations."

He nodded, so I stepped aside. I watched Kai as he stared

at the sky as if he was doing something special. It was fucked up, this constant need I felt to look at him or be around him. I'd never thought I couldn't feel this; I just didn't want to let myself, but it seemed I didn't have a choice with him. It would end because most relationships—did I even call this a relationship?—most of them did. Our lives were going in different directions, which was completely normal, but as I rubbed a hand over my left pec, I realized it would hurt.

"Wow. I didn't do too bad. It's really clear."

"You did good," I told him, and Kai beamed at me, making the thumping beneath the palm on my chest increase.

Time passed while I searched for constellations, and each time I found one, I showed it to Kai and told him about it. I was surprised I remembered as much as I did, surprised we were spending time this way instead of fucking each other's brains out. That's what I was used to doing with men, but like he had so many things, Kai shook my world apart in this too.

He was beautiful as he peeked through the telescope, robe open, the moon and the balcony lights creating a sort of spotlight on him. My skin prickled with heat, and suddenly, I didn't want to look at the stars anymore. I just wanted to look at him.

"Hey," I said, my voice coming out raspier than intended. Kai turned to me, a spark in his eyes when he realized what I wanted. He stood up straight, smiling at me. "Take off the robe."

I didn't have to tell him twice. Kai immediately let it fall from his shoulders. He stood in front of me, cock already at half-mast. Trim muscles ran the length of his body, his flat stomach rising and falling. He took me in as I did the same to him. I wanted to pull on the piercings in his nipples with my teeth, wanted to lick him from head to toe, suck his cock, and bury myself deep in his ass.

"You like what you see, baby?" he asked, and damned if his confidence didn't turn me on even more.

"Turn around."

He did, then peeked over his shoulder at me. His ass was so fucking fine—tight, plump globes I loved pushing between.

I let my robe fall, my dick hard and ready for him, and Kai inhaled a sharp breath. I walked over to him, rubbed my groin against his ass, kissing his neck and shoulders. My arms twined around him as I plucked at his piercings. "You gonna be good for me tonight? Let me show you how much I appreciate what you did for me?"

He leaned back against me, his body damn near melting into mine. "Yes. Fuck yes."

My left hand traveled down his torso while my right continued to play with his nipples. "What if I want to bind your wrists? Tie you to the futon so I can do whatever I want to you?"

His whole body vibrated against me, quick panting breaths puffing past his lips when I wrapped a hand around his cock and stroked. "You can do anything you want to me, Marcus."

"Hmmm." I licked his earlobe, then blew against it. "Ask me to do it. I want to hear you ask me to tie up your wrists."

"It's like part of me wants to argue, but the other would fucking beg because I'm dying for you."

I smiled into his neck. "Ask me, baby boy. I won't do it until you do."

"Please tie me up."

"That's what I want to hear. Lie on the futon." I backed away from him and went into my room.

"Lube and condoms are already out here. I was prepared!" Kai called after me, making me laugh.

I went into my closet and got a tie because that was all I

had to use on him. If he was up for this kind of play, we'd definitely have to get some toys, and—

He's not staying… He'll be leaving soon…

Something about that thought made me grab a second tie.

When I got back on the balcony, Kai was lying on his back, smiling at me while stroking his erection.

"Did I say you could touch yourself?"

"No, but technically you didn't say I couldn't either."

"Such a fucking troublemaker." It was one of my favorite things about him. "Put your arms over your head."

"Then I can't jack my dick."

"You're the one who asked for this."

He grinned. "Why is Bossy Marcus so hot?"

"All Marcuses are hot." I winked. Kai raised his arms, and I straddled his chest, wrapping one of the ties around his wrists before binding it to the futon's wooden frame. "Is this too tight?"

"No."

"Tell me if you get too uncomfortable and need me to take it off."

He nodded, mischief in his deep-brown eyes when he motioned toward my dick bobbing in front of him. "Can I have that now, please? Like you said earlier, I'm hungry for it."

"Be patient." I gave myself a stroke just to taunt him.

He whimpered. "Not fair. I'm being good."

"You are…but that doesn't mean I'm going to give you what you want."

I picked up the second tie. My dick was leaking, and I wanted nothing more than to bury it in his mouth the way he'd asked, but instead I said, "I'm going to blindfold you. If it's okay, ask me. If it's not, I won't."

He swallowed, then said, "Will you blindfold me?"

"So fucking naughty," I teased before wrapping it around his head. The second I had his eyes covered, I missed looking into them, the way they sparked with whatever he was feeling—horny, ornery, sweet…

"Shit…it's crazy not being able to see or touch you. I feel vulnerable."

"In a good way or a bad way?"

"Good…because it's you."

That's what I wanted to hear. I pushed up onto my knees, edging myself forward until my balls rested over his mouth. "Lick my sac, baby boy."

"Fucking finally." Kai lashed his tongue over my nuts, making my blood sizzle in the best way. He sucked them, kissed them, fucking made love to them like they were his favorite goddamned thing in the world.

Uncover his eyes, look at him…

But I didn't. I just let him taste, press his face into my balls and my taint, while my body fucking trembled.

"Marcus!" he said when I pulled back.

"I'm not going anywhere. Just gonna give you some dick. You want that, right?"

"Yes. God yes." He arched off the futon, trying to get to me, but I stayed out of reach. Precum pearled at my slit, so I leaned closer, tracing his lips, painting them with it.

When I pulled back, Kai licked it from his mouth before smirking and saying, "More, please…only this time can I have your cock too?"

How could I say no to that?

I angled my dick toward his mouth and pushed inside. His lips stretched, but he took me well. There was nothing sexier than a naked Kai, tied up and swallowing my cock.

I made short thrusts, working him into it before I fucked his mouth. He moaned, writhed beneath me, but I could tell it was because he loved this and wanted more. Still, I pulled out. "You good?"

"Fucking perfect."

God, he was great.

I didn't go as easy on him this time, my hips snapping forward. Kai swallowed around my cock. A tear slipped out from under the blindfold. I wiped it with my thumb, wanting nothing more than to unload my balls down his pretty throat, but I had more in store for us.

"You like that?" I rubbed my wet dick all over his face. Drool ran down one side of his mouth.

"Yes...don't stop."

"But I want to suck you now. Gonna lick and kiss my way down your body before I blow you too."

Kai thrust upward like he couldn't stop himself. I smiled, kissed his swollen lips, then down his throat, stopping to suck and bite at his nipples before working my way down his body.

I wanted to treat him like the king he was, the way he'd made me feel tonight.

When I got to his groin, I probed his slit with my tongue, then nursed his crown.

"Marcus...you don't even know." He tugged at the tie on his wrists, but it didn't come free.

"Look at this cock, leaking for me. So fucking thick." My tongue traveled from his balls to the tip. I nuzzled his balls, inhaled his scent, licked sweat and chlorine from his skin. I loved the way he tasted, how he smelled like me and my hot tub and lust. His cock stretched out my lips and was hot against my tongue as I showed him how much I wanted him.

Pulling off, I sucked my fingers, then swallowed him down again while I worked open his tight hole with one, then two digits.

Kai pumped his hips, shook his head, looked like he was

trying to get the blindfold off while he fucked my mouth.

"You good?" I asked.

"So good. Fuck me."

I wanted that, but there was something else I wanted too. "Do you top?"

Kai froze beneath me. "I...yes... You're gonna give me your hole?"

"No. I'm gonna take your cock."

He laughed. "Always in control."

What he didn't know was I'd never felt so out of control in my life.

"I want to see you."

"I'll take it off if you want." But I didn't want that. It was my hang-up. I bottomed from time to time, so it wasn't that, just...it felt like too much tonight.

"We're good. It's kinda cool losing two of my senses. Makes the others sharper."

"Thank you." I kissed his hip.

A row of condoms and a bottle of lube sat beside the futon. I grabbed them both and set them on the cushions next to me.

I slicked my fingers, kissing his balls and nuzzling his groin while I worked myself open—one digit, then two and three. It was uncomfortable at first, like it always was, but it helped to listen to him breathe and hear him whisper, "I can't wait to be inside you. I'm more of a bottom, but I'm dying to fuck you, Marcus. Never wanted anyone more."

It was killing me to wait, so I opened a rubber, rolled it down his prick, and once it was slick with lube, I straddled him. I held his cock with one hand as I lowered my ass down on it. There was pressure, but damned if my eyes didn't roll back because I wanted this with him.

"Marcus...baby...so good. I'm not gonna last. Jesus,

you're tight. I can't believe you're letting me have your hole."

That was all I needed to lower the rest of the way down, impaling myself on his dick.

I rode Kai while he arched and whimpered and begged for more. My dick had softened some, but as he worked me, rubbing my prostate, I got hard again.

"Look at you, letting me have your dick when I want it. You're so fucking fine, baby boy. Never wanted a cock more."

"Oh God!" he cried out, snapping his hips. His dick spasmed inside me, his body tight as he gave himself to his orgasm.

The second he went limp on the cushions, I said, "I need your hole."

I sheathed up, lubed my prick, then tugged the blindfold off him. Kai looked dazed, but a small smile curled his lips as he said, "Fuck me, baby."

I pulled his legs over my shoulders and thrust into him in one swift movement. I jackhammered into him, getting drunk off the suction of his ass on my dick. He was so fucking tight, I wanted to be inside him all night, but I needed to blow my load too.

"Kiss me," he asked, and I did, tongue pushing into his mouth as I pumped into him over and over again until my world splintered apart. A growl started deep in my chest, falling from my lips when I lost the fight with my orgasm and spilled into the condom.

Kai smiled at me again before closing his eyes. "That was hands down the best sex I've ever had. I can't move. I don't want to move. I might die."

I chuckled, untying his wrists. He still had the condom on, so I took that off. Cum ran down his groin, and I licked it up—because why the fuck not?—then tossed both rubbers in the trash can.

"Don't go," Kai said when I went for the open glass doors.

"Just gonna clean us up."

"I don't want to be cleaned up. I want to smell like sex the rest of the night."

Fuck, he was going to kill me.

I got back on the futon with him, grabbed the blankets, and covered us up.

Kai fell right asleep, but I stayed awake most of the night, watching him.

Chapter Twenty-Two
Kai

"I CAN CUT your hair for you if you want," I said to Marcus a few days later when we were about to start getting ready to go see my folks.

He cocked a brow, which was clearly his thing. "Are you saying I need a haircut?"

"No, but yesterday you told me you wanted to get one, that you've been too busy because you work too much and have been working even more because you feel guilty that you've been enjoying your life so much."

I'd been coming to his room after work every night, and we slept together and fucked and were both very careful not to mention that I'd told Marcus I liked him and that he'd admitted to liking me too—which I still couldn't fucking believe.

Marcus stalked over to me, wearing nothing but a pair of boxer trunks, and pressed me against the counter. "Don't put words in my mouth. None of that stuff about work or enjoying my life came from me."

"Don't try to sound all demanding and annoyed when I know you're not."

He grinned, and I wasn't sure there was anything in the world better than when I made Marcus smile. "You know how demanding I can be…" He ground his groin against mine. I refused to get hard and sidetrack us, so I put a hand on his chest and gently pushed him back.

"Be good."

"Baby boy, I'm always good."

Fuck. There went my dick. "Stop that! You're going to make me want to have sex with you. We're getting ready, and we're going to see my folks."

He groaned. "Why do I always listen to you? Clippers are under the sink. Let me get a chair."

I couldn't pretend it didn't give me the warm fuzzies that Marcus seemed to have a different set of rules when it came to me. I tried not to let myself believe it meant this would go anywhere. I would take a page out of his book and be a realist. Our differences and the long distance and a million other things meant that what we had now was all we ever would, but…

Holy shit. For the first time in my life, I wanted a relationship. How in the hell had that happened?

I grabbed the supplies, and then Marcus returned with a stool and sat down. "Which length?"

He handed over the attachments and told me what he liked.

The familiar *buzz* filled the air, and it didn't take me long to clean up his neck and fix his fade. There was something really fucking hot about sitting in his bathroom with him, doing his hair. Strangely, it felt almost as intimate as fucking, though it wasn't as if I'd never done someone's hair before. I could corn row or put in box braids. I used to help Mom braid Faith's hair when I was younger. Later, I'd made extra money doing hair for people in my old neighborhood, but it had never felt like it did with Marcus.

"All done." I kissed his cheek, then exaggeratedly gagged in the sink. "I think I ate some of your hair."

He rolled his eyes, but he enjoyed this. "You're a fool."

"Thanks, baby." I winked.

We cleaned up the mess real quick, then got in the shower together.

"I'll moisturize your scalp," I said when we got out.

"I can do it."

"Never said you couldn't."

For a moment I thought he was going to shut me down, but he nodded and sat for me so I could take care of him. I loved doing things like this for Marcus, which was a bit of a shock to the system.

We finished getting ready, and like always, he kept that slight bit of stubble on his face that I loved against my skin.

Before I knew it, we were in Marcus's car.

"The ten, to the sixty, seventy-one, then the ninety-one," I said. "I know the route like the back of my hand, and even if it tells you traffic is better the other way, it's usually not."

"I hate the ninety-one," Marcus replied.

"Who doesn't? I hate every freeway, but it's part of life."

It took an hour and a half to get there, but everything took forever in Southern California. We were used to it.

We'd just pulled onto the street I grew up on when I said, "Thank you for having my back today. My mom's gonna be hurt, especially since it took me so long to tell her, but I just... I don't want to let her down, but I've also got to do what I think is right, ya know?" I shrugged. "So yeah, I appreciate it. This is probably going to be a mess. It's that house."

I pointed to the older, peach-colored stucco home. Marcus pulled off onto the side of the road, hooked his finger beneath my chin, and turned my head so I faced him. "You don't let them down. I hear how the two of you talk on the phone. It's like you're best friends or something. She's just going to miss you."

Yeah, he was right. I knew that, and damn, I wanted Marcus to have what I did. I knew my mama would take him in, though. "She'll kick my ass for not telling her sooner."

"That too," he joked.

"I'm gonna miss you," tumbled out of my mouth.

He cocked his head slightly before lowering his hand. His reply didn't come straight away, but his gaze didn't turn from me. It lured me in, spoke the words Marcus didn't say aloud—*I'm gonna miss you too.* "We should go in. No stalling."

I nodded, and the two of us headed for the door. The metal screen door was closed, but the front door was open, voices drifting outside.

I pulled it open just as I heard, "Uncle Kai!" before the babies came running for me.

"They like me," I told Marcus, who stepped in behind me.

"Who's that?" Lil Jay asked.

"This is my friend Marcus."

"He's tall," my nephew replied.

"Jay…" my brother said from across the room. He was big on teaching the kids about respect.

My nephew held his hand out to Marcus. "Hi, I'm Jalen."

"What's up, lil man? I'm Marcus." He knelt, and they shook. The other kids all tried to do the same, telling him their names and giving him their hands.

I'd never seen Marcus with kids before. I couldn't pretend part of me didn't want to just sit back and enjoy it—the man who was usually gruff with people he didn't know was the complete opposite with them.

Mama and Faith came out of the kitchen, just as my dad, brother, and the spouses stood. When Marcus was on his feet,

Jalen approached him. "How old are you?"

"Jay," I warned just as my dad swatted the back of his head.

"Old enough that I don't have to answer that question, just like Kai is old enough that he doesn't need you to worry about that on his behalf," Marcus replied, and...oh shit. Marcus was letting my brother know that our relationship was between us. All I could do was hold my breath.

Jalen smiled. "I like him. What's up, man?" And just like that, I knew Jalen and Marcus would be okay.

"Nice to meet you, son. I'm Bernard," Dad introduced himself.

"And I'm Ann." Mama hugged him, then introduced the rest of the family. It was a lot of names, but Marcus struck me as the kind of man who would remember them all.

Everyone went to take a seat in the living room, but there weren't a lot of them. The couch was full. I was going to sit on the floor so Marcus could have the last chair, but he shook his head. "I'm good. Sit down."

I almost argued with him, but I knew Marcus would insist, which would draw more attention, so I said playfully, "Thanks, baby." I felt the eyes of everyone in my family on me, but I ignored them.

He went right down on the carpet, which surprised me. I'd never seen Marcus sit on the floor in my life, and when my family all tried to offer him a seat, he said no, thank you.

He was close to me, his arm touching my leg... *Oh*...Marcus *wanted* to be close to me, maybe even needed it, and that played all sorts of tricks with my heart.

"So what do you do?" Faith asked.

"I'm in real estate—residential and commercial both."

"And your family? They around here?" Mama asked.

"They're architects. They're originally from the high

desert, up toward Victorville, but ended up in LA after high school, put themselves through school and all that."

"You didn't want to follow in their footsteps?" Dad asked.

"I have a degree in architecture, but I wanted to make my own way."

I laid a hand on his nape, brushing my fingers against his skin. Every adult in the room noticed, but I didn't pull away. I wanted to support him when he was talking about his parents. No way would we make it through this day without the third degree, even if they thought we were just friends. That's not how we rolled.

"And how did you and Kai meet?" Faith asked next.

"I told you. He's close with Declan, who owns Driftwood."

"It's fine," Marcus said, letting me know he didn't feel like they were asking too many questions.

"Are you Uncle Kai's boyfriend?" Lil Jay asked. "Dad said Uncle Kai likes boys and that's okay."

I chuckled. Marcus's gaze shot to me, slightly panicked. I rolled my eyes, hoping he could tell I was calling him a big baby. "Marcus is my best friend," I told him. When I looked at Marcus again, his eyes weren't as panicked, and instead, everything about him had softened, like I had somehow said the most perfect thing without knowing it.

It was true. Maybe it had only been a short time, and yeah, we were sleeping together and said we liked each other, but Marcus had also become the closest friend I ever had. No one had ever made me feel as important and cared for as he did.

"Aww!" Jalen's wife, Lissa, and Faith said at the same time.

Funny, that was how I felt inside every time I looked at Marcus.

THE REALIST

★ ★ ★

"Scrambled eggs!" Marcus shouted at me as I was drawing in a family game of Pictionary.

"Yes! My baby's smart!" I teased, then realized how it sounded and that I probably shouldn't act with my family the way I would with Marcus at home.

"Just friends, huh?" Jalen said.

"I'm ignoring you."

Marcus was in one of the chairs now, and he tugged me into his lap. We'd been here for hours already. We'd eaten, talked, shot hoops in the backyard, and now we were playing games.

Marcus was completely at ease in a way that had surprised me. My family had been great, and they treated him like their own—equal parts giving him shit and smothering him the way they did with me.

God, I was going to miss them.

I still hadn't told them I was moving. The longer the day went, the harder it became, but I knew it was something I had to do, so when the game ended and Mama said she was going to the kitchen to get dessert ready, I said, "I'll help."

The house wasn't open concept, so we would have some privacy there. I knew she had to be the first person I told.

"I like him a lot," was the first thing she said when we were behind the kitchen door.

"He's a good man," I replied when what I really wanted to say was that I liked him too.

"He's crazy about you. I can tell."

"It's not serious."

"Yeah, that's what I said about your daddy when we met, and look at us now."

I'd be lucky to have a relationship like theirs, but then I

remembered it would never happen and what I was there to tell her. "I need to talk to you about something."

Concern creased her brow. "What is it?"

"Don't be upset, please...and I know I should have told you earlier but, well, I'm an idiot and was being a baby. Anyway, I really think this is a smart, adult move for me, which is what I know you want for me and..." And I was rambling.

"What's going on, Kai?"

"I got offered a job, running a brand-new bar myself, and a really great apartment at an amazing price. The only thing is, it's in Atlanta."

"I don't know an Atlanta in Southern California, but you'd better not be talking about Georgia."

I smiled because that was so her. "Maybe this is the kind of offer I've been waiting for. There aren't a whole lot of options. I can't stay with Marcus forever, which means I'd have to come back home and I'd lose my job. I just... I have to do this. I have to try, at least. You're all so settled, and I'm...not."

"What about Marcus?" Mama asked.

"I told you, we're not serious. We're...something, but he knows I'm leaving, and I doubt it would go anywhere if I wasn't. He's got his shit together. Eventually he'd get annoyed with me."

"Kai Lewis, don't you talk about my son that way. You're smart and beautiful and perfect, and if he doesn't see that, it's on him, but the way that man in there was watching you? He's not getting tired of a damn thing, and he never will."

If only the world could see me the way my mama did. My heart stumbled at the thought of Marcus doing so.

"Even if that's true, it doesn't fix everything. I'm paying him to rent a room—less than I should for what I have—and he's only taking the money because I insisted. I work for his best friend. I can't afford a new car or my own apartment. I'm not a real catch. Marcus deserves someone who doesn't have to mooch off him."

"So you're just going to leave? Drop everything and move across the country where you have no real friends or family to take an opportunity that sounds too good to be true?"

"It's Archer. You remember him. He moved a few years back. He's doing well in Atlanta."

She crossed her arms. "I don't like or trust that boy."

"Okay, but I need you to trust me."

Mama sighed, a tear spilling from her eye before she wiped it away. "You're already too far away. I can't imagine having you across the country. How will I survive it?"

"Pfft. Do you know you? You're the strongest person I know. And I'll visit all the time. You're my family, and that's not going to change." She nodded, and I pulled her into a hug. "I love you. I'm doing this because you raised me to be strong and to want to stand on my own. That's what I'm trying to learn how to do."

"I love you too." I held her for a moment while she cried, but it was Mama who pulled away first, swiping at her tears. "How long?"

"I'm thinking about a month now." That's what Archer said, but he hadn't given an exact date. He'd been busy getting it all set up lately, so he didn't have as much time to talk.

"You'll be great! Managing a bar on your own is big."

And just like that, she had my back, the way parents were supposed to. "Thank you. Part of why I brought Marcus today is because he doesn't have this. His family isn't close the way we are, so thanks for accepting him and making him feel at home. I know it sounds weird, but I wondered if we could find a way for you to keep doing it? Get his number and just reach out sometimes?" My heart twitched uncomfortably, though I couldn't put my finger on why.

Mama's expression softened, and she smiled. "Oh, Kai. You love him."

I shrugged. I didn't know if I did or not, but I *something-ed* him.

When I didn't speak, she added, "It's going to be hard for you to leave him—harder than leaving us."

"That doesn't mean I don't have to. I don't even know if Marcus would want more from me, but if he did, he would do everything he could to take care of me." Marcus enjoyed it, that much was clear, and in some ways, it would work for both of us. I couldn't pretend I didn't like him doing some of the things he did, but I didn't want him to *have* to. When it came to money, I didn't want to depend on Marcus at all. There was a difference between us enjoying playing roles and *having* to live by them.

"I'm proud of you, Kai. Always." She pulled me down and kissed my forehead just as there was a noise behind us. We turned around as Marcus opened the door.

"Sorry, I didn't mean to interrupt. I just wanted to see if there's anything I can do to help?"

No, he wanted to make sure I didn't need him. A sharp stab pierced my gut. Oh God. My mom was right. How in the hell had I let myself fall in love with Marcus? And how was I ever going to leave him?

I grabbed his wrist and tugged him to me, wrapping my arms around his shoulders. "Everything is okay," I said softly before pressing my lips to his.

Mama mumbled a soft, "It's not serious," behind us before she asked, "How about you help us get these pies out and cut, and then the three of us will go and tell the rest of the family Kai's good news?"

That's exactly what we did, her on one side of me, Marcus on the other.

Chapter Twenty-Three

Marcus

KAI'S MOM HAD texted me twice since we'd been at their house the week before. She'd asked for my number before we left. I had a feeling Kai had something to do with it. While that should have made me feel…I didn't know—frustrated? Like shit? Needy?—it just made me appreciate him more. The man had fucked with my head, and I wasn't sure how to handle it.

But his family was great. I liked them a lot. They'd taken me in, all of them, and when Kai had announced his decision to move, even though they were clearly worried and would miss him, they all made sure Kai knew they would support him all the way. They not only told him how much they loved him, they *showed* it.

That was something else that had been on my mind all damned week.

Kai was at work, so I knew I'd be going home to an empty house. I'd seen Corb on Sunday when we'd recorded the latest episode of *The Vers*, but we hadn't spent much one-on-one time together lately. That made me feel like shit. Corbin had always been my person, and I didn't want to let that slide because I was feeling some kinda thing for Kai.

I called him before heading home from the office. Corbin answered on the second ring. "Miss me?"

"Like a hole in the head," I teased, then said, "I figured it's been a while since you were blessed with my company. Come have dinner at my house tonight and help me edit the last episode of *The Vers*."

"It's okay if you miss me and just want to spend time with me, Daddy M. It doesn't make you less gruff and badass. I'll be right there."

I had to force myself not to laugh. "Asshole."

"Your favorite one! Oh, wait. That sounded weird. You know what I meant."

This time I let myself chuckle before ending the call. I got home and showered, putting on a pair of sweats and no shirt after. When I got downstairs, Corbin was in the living room. "I ordered food. I knew you'd be all Marcus about me eating."

He was on his phone, sitting at the bar. I walked over and plucked the cell from his hand. "None of this tonight."

"You know you're not really my dad, right? You're not the boss of me, Marcus!" He crossed his arms, his words and actions purposefully dramatic.

"Give social media a break."

"What if I was on Grindr?"

"You don't need to hook up tonight. You're with me."

"Yeah, but you don't give me orgasms," he joked.

"You couldn't handle me." I winked.

"Would be like sleeping with my brother, but…now that we're on the subject…you and Kai…" He waggled his brows. "You gonna pull a Declan and Parker and fall in love? What the fuck is up with us? We managed to make it into our thirties without falling into the heteronormative trap of a monogamous relationship, and now I'm the last man standing."

I nearly choked on my tongue. Don't ask me how, but I did. "I'm not in love with Kai." That would be a disaster.

Completely ridiculous. I would never... My pulse took off like the start of a race. What the fuck. Was I in love with Kai? I didn't know how to even do that. Plus, there was no possibility it would last. I was too smart to let myself do something that dumb.

Corbin nearly fell off the barstool laughing.

"You're a damn fool," I said, thankfully saved by the doorbell.

I went to answer it, Corbin still cracking up behind me.

I hated my friend.

I went to the door, and there was Japanese food in a bag waiting for me. I brought it in, set it on the counter, and got plates. "I don't love him."

"Okay." Finally, he'd calmed down. "You met his family..."

"Not as his boyfriend. I went to support Kai."

"Oh, you mean like you'd do for me, Park, or Dec if we needed you? Because you *love* us, which is how you feel about him, only you also get to stick your penis inside him, which is basically a relationship from what I've gathered—love, friendship, and sex. Hmm, maybe that wouldn't be so bad. Maybe I should try and find me one of those boyfriend things."

It was my turn to laugh. In some ways he was an idiot, but he was also the best in every way. "We're not boyfriends," I said, not looking at him as I transferred our fried rice and teriyaki chicken to plates. Corbin took them to the table while I opened a bottle of wine, bringing that and two glasses over. "He's twenty-six."

"So? Jesus, Marcus. He's a functioning adult. Who the fuck cares if you're old and he's not?"

I sat beside him. "If I'm old, then you're old."

"I'm good regardless." He blew me a kiss.

I sighed. Fuck, what was I doing? Why in the hell was I even talking about this? I'd completely lost it—had a personality transplant or some shit. I wanted the old me back. "He's moving."

"Ask him to stay." Corbin took a bite of his food. I was thankful I didn't have to push him to do so. Most of the time he was okay, but he got into funks where he was so scared of gaining weight, he would hardly eat.

"I can't ask him to stay. I would never do that. It's not fair to him. He sees this as his chance of making something of his life. He's trying to figure out what he wants and to find his own way in the world the same way I did when I was younger. I would never ask him to sacrifice that because I'm…" I waved my hands. "Feeling him. He would resent me." God, this sucked. Why did we have to discuss this? Couldn't we pretend none of it was happening?

He cocked his head, the expression on his face changing, the corners of his mouth turned down. I didn't know if he even realized he did it. "Then go with him," Corbin said softly. "If you wouldn't want to leave because of me, you can, Marcus. I'd be fine. I'd miss you, and I'd have to have my own room in your Atlanta house so I could come stay with you whenever I wanted, but I'd be fine, and oooh! You and Kai could adopt me! Then I'd have two daddies."

He meant for me to laugh, but I didn't. I couldn't leave Santa Monica. Why would he even say that? Especially for something that Kai and I hadn't even put a name to. He was going to learn about himself, and the last thing I wanted was to drag him down or keep him from figuring it all out. "That's ridiculous."

"No, it's not. If you love him, it's not."

"It would never work."

"You're making excuses. You're not your parents. You're

better at loving people than anyone I know, Marcus. You deserve to be happy, and if Kai makes you feel that way, if he really makes you *feel* it, then you have to do everything you can to hold on to it."

What about you?

I didn't need to speak the words for Corbin to know they were there. "We'll never change. You'll never get rid of me. If I needed you, I have no doubt you would jump on a plane and be here for me the moment you could, but I can't spend my life depending on you…coming to you when I need to feel better about myself."

"You don't do that," I said, but we both knew he did, and that had always worked for us. Corbin needed me more than even Parker and Declan did, and I needed to be needed. It was strictly platonic, but that didn't change what we were to each other. When Corbin stared at me like I was an idiot, I said, "I'm not in love with him, and I'm not leaving. I don't even know why we're talking about this. I like him. There's no denying that, but my life is here, and Kai is trying to get independence. I wouldn't ever take that away from him."

Corbin rolled his eyes, but he let it go. We finished eating and talked about safe subjects that had nothing to do with Kai. After dinner we worked on editing *The Vers*. I still kept Corbin's phone, and the fact that he didn't ask for it back told me he'd been obsessing about his social media pages and knew he needed a break.

"Let's watch a show," I said, and he nodded. We settled on the couch, and I found a comedy I knew he'd like.

"Did I tell you I have a new neighbor? His name is Spencer, and he hates me."

I turned to face him. "Fuck him. Not literally. Or did you already?"

Corbin chuckled. "I didn't fuck him. He says I'm conceited and, I quote, believe looks matter more than anything else. That I'm spreading a dangerous narrative to younger queer youth about their bodies and appearance. What the fuck is that? Who the hell does he think he is? Spencer doesn't know shit about me."

"Jesus. Don't listen to him. You're not listening to him, right?"

Corbin shrugged.

"Corb. Seriously, fuck that guy. Don't listen to him. He doesn't know you."

"He's on the thicker side...a little softer, or fuller. We got into it, and he said I would never date someone like him because he doesn't have the perfect body—his words, not mine. Which isn't fucking true. I'm not *that* superficial. But then...look how I am with that fucking phone. I'm always obsessing about it, scanning comments and freaking the fuck out over everything people say. I can't help wondering...is he right about me?"

Furious heat scorched my body. Whoever the hell this Spencer was, he needed to cut this shit out. I'd find him myself and tell him to. "Hey," I said. When Corbin didn't look at me, I held his chin and turned his head toward me. "He doesn't know you, kid. It sounds like he's projecting some of his own shit on you. He doesn't know who you are. You love everyone. It's yourself you can't seem to feel the same way about." When I pulled him close, Corbin came easily. I wrapped an arm around him and kissed his temple. "I love you, kid."

"I love you too."

We sat there for a while, eventually ending up with Corbin's head in my lap and my feet resting on the coffee table. I ran my fingers through his dark hair while we pretended to watch a show neither of us gave a shit about, and it wasn't long before Corbin fell asleep.

It was late when I heard the door open. I turned my head and pressed a finger to my lips, then pointed down. Kai frowned but was quiet as he came closer, peeking over the couch to see Corbin.

It took a moment for everything to register and for me to wonder if this was something I shouldn't do anymore. Corbin was my person, but Kai was…Kai was my person in a different way. I didn't want to hurt him, but I couldn't not be who Corbin needed from me either.

"It's not," I said softly. Fuck, I'd never explained myself to a man, but I needed to with Kai. "We're not… He was having a hard night."

I could see the wheels turning in his head, as if at first he wasn't sure what I was saying, but then he smiled. He kissed my cheek, then knelt behind the couch, mouth close to my ear. "Baby…this right here, what you're doing with Corbin, is one of my favorite things about you. I would never ask you to change. You're not Marcus if you're not the best friend in the world to those you love. It just makes me like you more."

My heart thumped against my chest. Blood rushed through my ears to the point where everything in the background sounded muffled.

That was perfect. He was fucking everything I hadn't known I wanted or needed.

Holy fuck, I was in love with Kai, and I didn't know what to do about it.

Chapter Twenty-Four

Kai

I FELT MARCUS get out of bed the next morning. Usually, I ignored that shit, but something made me get up today. He was quiet when he went into the bathroom, trying not to disturb me. I pulled on a pair of pajama pants and made my way downstairs, wondering if Corbin was up. I figured he had to go to work too.

Marcus had gently sneaked out from beneath him last night and had brought him a blanket. When I asked why he didn't wake him up to go to the spare room, he said he worried Corbin would make him give him his phone back and leave. If Marcus kept it, Corbin wouldn't go without it. I didn't know what that was about, but I trusted that if Marcus had it, he had a good reason.

When I got downstairs, Corbin was sitting on the couch. He looked up at me with sleep-ruffled hair. "I'm going to kick your boyfriend's ass. He stole my cell."

"I heard. He's in the shower. You can try to beat him up when he gets out. Until then, want some breakfast?" I rubbed a hand over my face, trying to wake up. Getting up early sucked.

Corbin frowned. "You don't have to cook breakfast for me."

"I know, but I'm a nice guy who likes to show off his mad

kitchen skills," I teased. Corbin surprised me by following me over.

"Listen..." He sat on a barstool. "I, um...hope I didn't make you uncomfortable last night. With Marcus. He's my family. That's all it is."

Okay, well, that was maybe one of the sweetest things I ever heard. Corbin didn't have to say anything like that to me, but I appreciated the thought. "Marcus isn't mine. We're just..." I let the sentence hang in the air because I wasn't sure how to finish it.

He laughed to the point that I picked up an apple from the basket on the counter and threw it at him. Corbin caught it and took a bite.

"What's so funny?"

"You...saying Marcus isn't yours. If you believe that, you don't know him."

I ignored what he was saying—no way it was true—and got eggs out of the fridge. "I'll make some eggs with veggies and oatmeal. It's gross, but Marcus likes oatmeal a ton."

"He's never been like this with anyone before. I just... Don't hurt him, Kai. He would never let you know if you did, but he'd feel it deeper than you can imagine."

I paused, halfway to the counter, eggs in my hands and my feet suddenly rooted to the floor. How did he think I could hurt Marcus? Yeah, he'd said he liked me, but I couldn't imagine it being that much.

"Are you drunk?" I tried to play it off like that was the excuse for what he'd said.

"Wow. Stealing a page out of my book now, are we?"

"Hey, I cover emotions with sarcasm and jokes too. You don't own that."

Corbin and I both chuckled, but then he sobered. "Don't let him run away. Don't let him pretend this doesn't matter to him. There's no one who deserves to be fought for more than Marcus because he would go to the ends of the earth for the people he loves."

Words stuck in my mouth, my throat tight and my stomach suddenly full and heavy. I didn't know how to respond to that, what to say. He was right. Marcus did deserve that, and he *would* do anything for the people he loved. "Even if he wanted more from me, what do I bring to the table? I'm too loud, too much, not responsible enough, and can barely take care of myself without depending on him, my old roommate, or my parents. I can't give him anything."

Corbin shrugged. "He wouldn't want anything but you. Marcus doesn't give a shit about that other stuff."

"But I do…and he should. I want to be able to give him things too."

"Then find another way to make it work with him. If you're not willing to try, maybe I was wrong about you."

Before I could respond, the sound of Marcus's footsteps came from the stairs.

"Give me my phone before I skip work and hug you all day! You won't be able to go anywhere without me attached to you!" Corbin pushed over the stool and ran at Marcus, who looked horrified.

"Fuck that shit." He held the phone out to Corbin, both of them laughing before he kissed Corbin's temple and said something quiet, only for the two of them.

Corbin nodded in return.

Marcus looked my way and winked before walking over and saying, "I couldn't believe my bed was empty when I got out of the shower." He wrapped his arms around me from behind and kissed my neck. He did it because he wanted to make sure I knew where I stood, that he wasn't only giving affection to Corbin, which was sweet and totally Marcus.

"None of that, Dads." Corbin gave us a mock-serious face.

"I'm making breakfast," I said.

"I'm going to head out," Corbin replied, which was when I noticed he wasn't wearing the same thing he'd had on last night.

"He has clothes in the spare room," Marcus answered, maybe seeing how I looked him up and down. Maybe he'd changed at some point in the middle of the night. Marcus turned to Corbin. "Eat, Kai is cooking."

"I don't know how you put up with his bossiness." Corbin plunked down on the stool again.

"I'll help you," Marcus told me, but I waved it off. I knew he didn't want to seem like he was saying I *had* to cook for them; but I'd just said I was, and he wanted Corbin to hang out for a bit first.

"It's okay. I got it. I like making food for you."

"Gag," Corbin said. "But also maybe a little cute. I can't believe I'm the last single member of *The Vers*. We should talk about how we're going to split custody of Marcus, especially if you move to Atlanta. That'll make things harder."

"Corbin." Marcus's voice was stern.

"Bet you're wishing you gave me my phone back last night so I left, huh?" he teased, the two of them going back and forth while I tried to work through what he'd said.

Was Corbin saying I shouldn't leave, or that he thought Marcus should go with me? I nearly laughed at that. Why in the hell would Marcus leave all this behind for me? Corbin had no idea what he was talking about.

"Be good, boys," I said, surprised I didn't sound like I was hyperventilating because it felt that way.

Corbin immediately got into his phone, and Marcus made coffee while I started breakfast. Before I knew it, I'd blanked at the whole breakfast and Marcus was turning on the fish tank lights and pretending he wasn't saying goodbye to the fish the way he always did. Blue had been back in the tank for a while now, living their best life.

"I'm outta here. I'll see you guys later," Corbin said. He gave me a quick hug, which I returned.

"Bye."

Marcus was next, and then Corbin was gone and it was just the two of us. "Thanks for feeding him and being chill with everything."

"How are you going to reward me?" I flirted, watching lust make his jaw twitch.

"I'll come to Driftwood tonight and fuck you in the bar. I know how much that turns you on."

I trembled. It really fucking did. "Deal." I winked. Marcus kissed me, and then he was gone too. I stood in the kitchen, trying to figure out what the fuck had happened in my life and what I was going to do about it.

★ ★ ★

I SPENT THE whole day thinking about what Corbin had said, and how he seemed to think Marcus felt about me, and the fact that I really fucking liked Marcus, but I was leaving him, not fighting for him. But staying made me feel like I wasn't fighting for myself either. It was all confusing as fuck.

"You okay? You seem a little off tonight," Declan said, making me realize I was standing behind the bar, spacing out.

"Yeah, fine. Just thinking." I'd sent Archer a text earlier, and I was waiting to hear back from him, which was something else that had me on edge.

"I probably don't want to know, do I?"

"Not unless you want to talk about how great a lay Marcus is," I teased, making Declan shake his head at me. It was all in good fun.

Declan looked over my shoulder and said, "Speak of the devil."

My heart did this strange acceleration thing for no reason as I turned around and saw Marcus come into the bar. It was a weeknight, so we weren't incredibly busy, but he definitely grabbed everyone's attention as he walked by. It was impossible not to notice Marcus, and clearly, I wasn't the only one who saw that.

He smiled. I pretended to swoon, and he quirked a brow the way he was known for doing before the edges of his lips curled up again.

"Holy shit," Declan said. "Corbin was right. I thought he was just being Corb."

What the fuck? Had Corbin immediately called Declan and Parker to tell them his insane hypothesis about Marcus and me? But as Marcus slid onto one of the stools, looking sexy and completely irresistible, I suddenly didn't care what Corbin had said.

"Hey, baby." I leaned over the counter. "So you really showed."

"I always do what I say I'm going to do."

"I have a feeling I'm not gonna like this," Declan added, and Marcus looked at him, giving Dec his attention.

"Gonna need your office."

"Again? What the fuck, Marcus. I hate this. It's weird." Declan stalked away, and the two of us chuckled.

"Hey, baby boy," Marcus said to me.

God, I loved it when he called me that. Why was it the sexiest thing I'd ever heard? "You had a lot of attention when you came in."

"You have a lot of attention all the time. Am I going to

have to show everyone in the bar tonight that you're mine?"

Oh, so he wanted to play that game. I was down for sure. "Maybe." I winked. "I should get to work."

I felt his gaze on me as I went to a group of guys. "Can I get you boys anything else?"

"You?" one of them joked. The other nudged him like he was embarrassed.

"Sorry. My friend is an idiot."

"It's okay, but I'm going to have to pass. He's my boyfriend." I pointed to Marcus, lying my ass off about who he was.

"Fuuuuuck. He's hot," the first guy said. "Threesome?"

"Nope. He likes to keep me all to himself. Drinks?"

I got a playful groan in return, someone called Marcus a lucky man, then me the same, which was definitely true. They didn't want anything more at the moment, so I made my rounds, playfully flirting but shooting glances at Marcus and making sure everyone knew I was his.

This game wasn't something I would've ever considered before, but I had to admit, it was hot. It clearly turned Marcus on to watch people want me and then claim me for himself. It made me feel wanted in a way I hadn't known I needed.

I headed back to the counter a little while later. Declan was busy with customers, and a new guy was sitting beside Marcus.

"He's fine, isn't he?" I heard Marcus say. For a moment, I thought he was talking to me about someone else, but his voice had been too low. When I turned to glance his way, I saw he was speaking to the guy.

"Fuck yes," he replied.

"I saw you watching him."

"Me and half the guys in here," the guy answered. I kept my back to them.

"Yeah, I noticed that too."

"There's also no doubt in my mind he's spoken for, unless you guys play?"

I turned when the guy finished speaking. I looked at Marcus, whose intense gaze was on me.

"Nah. I don't mind if you look, if you admire, but I don't share what's mine," he replied, and damned if that didn't send fire scorching up my spine.

"I don't share what's mine either," I added.

Before I realized what was happening, Marcus shoved to his feet, came around the counter, and picked me up, slinging me over his shoulder and making me laugh.

"Jesus Christ, Marcus," I heard Declan say, but he wore a supportive smile as Marcus apologized to him, then carried me to the back room.

The second I was on my feet, he tugged at my jeans until he'd pulled them down, and then bent me over Declan's desk. Lubed fingers pierced me, and then it was his slick, condom-covered cock pushing into my hole.

Marcus fucked me until I nearly lost my head, spurting my load all over my boss's desk, which I totally shouldn't be doing.

"Get back in me!" I said when he pulled out, but Marcus just ripped the condom off, came all over my ass, then rubbed it in again.

He kissed my neck, my back, and wrapped his arms around me from behind. "I want you to be mine," he said, breath against my ear. "Tell me you're really mine."

I was. It was scary and amazing at the same time. "I'm yours. I want…God, Marcus. I want to be your boyfriend." Somehow the word sounded too small, though, like it wasn't enough for what Marcus meant to me.

"Okay," he said as if it was just that easy. He kissed my

neck again. "I want that too."

"What about the rest of it?"

"We'll figure it out." Marcus pulled a towel out of thin air. Logically, he must have thought ahead and brought it with him. He cleaned me up, then my cum off the desk. Next, he pulled my underwear up, then my jeans, zipping and buttoning them for me. "I know you don't need it, but I still like to take care of you."

He did. That was just who he was. "I'm not complaining…most of the time. I just can't depend on you." Translation: that's what Atlanta was.

Marcus nodded.

"Can I tell everyone you're my boyfriend?"

"No."

"Okay, just Declan. And also Corbin because he called it this morning, which means we have to tell Parker. That automatically includes Sebastian and Elliott and—oh." He shut me up with his lips, tongue in my mouth like he owned me.

"Yes," Marcus said when he pulled away. "You know this is a fucking disaster waiting to happen, right?"

"So romantic."

"That's why I'm The Realist."

And maybe it was strange, but I loved him for it.

Chapter Twenty-Five
Marcus

"So...how's it feel having an official boyfriend?" Corbin asked in our next episode of *The Vers*.

"If you expect me to act a fool because you said that, you're gonna be waiting a long-ass time. I'm not Declan." I'd mentioned to them that Kai and I were together, then promptly started recording. Now I wasn't so sure that had been a smart plan.

"Hey!" Dec said. "What the fuck? How did I get pulled into this?"

Parker chimed in, "I agree that Marcus is being surprisingly chill about opening his heart and getting serious with another person for the first time."

"Especially because we know emotions and feelings aren't his favorite thing," Corb added. "I wonder if he provided Kai with a list of all the pros and cons of being in a relationship and then made two little squares at the bottom for him to check yes or no."

Oh fuck. Why had I even told them? But considering Kai, Elliott, and Sebastian were all waiting for us in the living room and this would be the first time we were all together since Kai and I had become official, I really didn't have much choice.

Or time to have a boyfriend... From the looks of things, he would be leaving in about three weeks, which was a week longer than we'd thought, but that was nowhere near enough.

"You're an idiot," I told Corbin.

"So you've told me eleven thousand times. I'm just saying, listeners, if you saw Marcus with his boyfriend, you'd be surprised too. He's so *doting*."

"I am not," I lied because I fucking was, and we all knew that shit.

"Oh my God, right?" Park asked. "It's so sweet."

"But then his voice gets deep and basically the verbal version of sex, and he's like…*Come here, baby boy, and give me that hole.*" Corbin waggled his brows.

"Jesus fucking Christ." I rubbed a hand over my face. "Why do I put up with you? And I can promise you, my ass has never said that in front of you."

"In front of you!" Parker shouted. "But you *have* said it. You heard it here first, *Vers* listeners."

I groaned, then shot a glance at Declan. "Why aren't you on my side here?"

He held up his hands. "Hey, don't look at me to save you. I'm still pissed about that I'm-not-Declan comment."

Fuck my life. "We're not talking about this anymore."

"We should invite Kai on the show," Declan said.

I gave him the finger. "I'm not playing this game with you guys." But I was and they knew it. Unfortunately, like Kai, they could get me to do anything.

"Okay, let's get serious for a minute," Parker interrupted, and by serious, I knew he meant he was going to say something from the heart. That was our Parker. "I know we joke around and tease each other a lot, but I just want to say how good it feels to be happy…and to see you guys happy. Sebastian is great, and I'm so happy Declan has him. Kai is incredible too, and he's the perfect match for Marcus." Except for the fact that he was leaving and we were going to have to be long-distance. But what was the alternative? I couldn't leave, and I could never expect Kai to stay for me. "And Elliott is the definition of sexy and the best husband ever."

"What the fuck? Bastian is sexy," Declan replied.

"Wait. Let me pull out my phone and video-record the two of you arguing about whose man is hotter." Corbin reached for his cell.

"Ha-ha," Parker added. "Next we just have to get Corb to fall for someone and—"

"If you finish that sentence, I swear we're not friends anymore, Parker Hansley-Weaver. I will not settle down ever!"

Declan cocked a brow. "Pretty sure that's what Marcus and I thought too."

"How about we continue the show now?" I said, reaching over to put my hand on Corbin's thigh. I didn't know if he needed it, but I was normally good at foreseeing these things. With all of us being coupled up now, I didn't want it to make him feel alone. "I was doing some research on queer history, and I found information on Bayard Rustin."

"I don't know that name," Parker said.

"Yeah, most people don't. This is the history we haven't been taught. Bayard Rustin was a queer activist who advised Reverend Martin Luther King Jr. He helped with the March on Washington, participated in Freedom Rides, and that's just the beginning. The sad part is because he was gay, he mostly worked behind the scenes." Which was shitty when you thought about it. "In the eighties he started doing more work for queer rights. He was posthumously awarded the Presidential Medal of Freedom in 2013. In 2020 he was pardoned by California's governor. He'd been arrested in 1953 because he was caught having sex with men. He had to register as a sex offender because of it."

"Shit," Dec said.

Corbin was shaking his head. "God, that shit is so fucked up."

Parker said, "It's important to remember and acknowledge the trailblazers. Without them, we wouldn't be sitting here doing this podcast right now." And he was right. We wouldn't.

We finished recording our episode, and once we'd shared information about our sponsors, I turned off the equipment. I didn't move because I knew we'd all have this out, and I'd rather do it with just the four of us than in front of Kai, Elliott, and Sebastian. "Let's get this over with," I said.

Parker sighed. "I want you to be happy. You and Kai are great together, but I'm worried you're gonna get hurt. He's leaving. You have your first real relationship at thirty-five, and it's long-distance?"

He was right. There was no doubt he was. Relationships were hard to make work in any circumstances, but add in the distance... I was smart enough to know we were doomed from the start.

I rested my elbows on the table, rubbing my eyes with one hand. "What do you think I should do? This is your territory, Park. I..." Loved Kai. I didn't know how to say that to them, though. I'd heard those three words from the men in this room more than from anyone else in my life, so if anyone would know, it would be them.

"Maybe he'll stay," Declan replied.

"But should he have to?" We all knew the reasons Kai had the right to leave and why he should.

After a few minutes of silence, Corbin said softly, "Why are we pretending Marcus couldn't go with him if he wanted to?"

Declan and Parker were silent, but my firm "No" echoed through the room.

"So it's okay to expect him to make a change and not you?" Corbin countered.

"I don't expect him to do shit. That's why I'm not asking him. You and I already went over this. It's not happening. Kai and I will do the long-distance thing for as long as it works, and that's that." The words alone felt like they were ripping apart my heart. I didn't know what our expiration date was, but I knew we had one.

"Don't do this for me, Marcus."

I groaned. "Jesus, Corb. Can we not have this discussion again?"

"I'm serious. I fucking know you. It would kill me if shit got fucked up with you guys because you feel some misplaced responsibility for me."

"Maybe he doesn't want me to go!" I said too loudly, and everyone in the room jumped. "He didn't ask. This is a really exciting time for him, Corb, so remember that's a real possibility too. He's starting a new life, and he deserves that. He wants to be on his own, and dragging his overbearing boyfriend with him isn't getting his independence. And I know you think it's just you—all of you—needing me, but…" How in the fuck did I even finish that sentence? As much as I loved them, as many times as I'd been there for them, I hadn't told them I needed them too.

One look around the room at the compassion and heart returned to me from each of their stares, and I knew I didn't have to. They knew.

"But you need him more, and that's okay," Corb said.

I didn't deny it, and no other words would come to me either. These men had been my world for so damn long, but now it had expanded to include Kai—Kai, whom I was in love with.

Corbin gave me a look that said he knew and understood.

My gaze went to Declan next, then Parker. None of them needed to say anything—I knew they supported me, that we would be okay and nothing would ever change with us, even if I left.

I thought about my parents, whom I rarely saw, and how I wondered if they were even in love with each other. I didn't want that. I wanted to know, and I wanted Kai to know too.

When they nodded, I saw that again—we didn't have to speak for them to see that if Kai wanted me, I would go with him. That there wasn't a damn thing I wouldn't do for the man who'd changed my world.

"I think this moment requires an extra-long Beach Bums hug," Corbin broke the silence, making us laugh, the way only he could do, and the tension dissipated. "I love you guys."

Corbin stood, tugged me to my feet, and wrapped his arms around me. I grumbled and complained the way I always did, but when Parker joined in, then Declan, I let myself feel it, enjoy it.

"I love you all too," Parker said.

"Love you," Declan added.

Mine was the loudest and steadiest of them all.

Chapter Twenty-Six

Kai

I KEPT TELLING myself not to freak out that Archer hadn't returned my phone calls over the last week and a half. I'd only called twice and texted once. He was a busy guy. He was preparing to get a new Midtown gay bar off the ground. And it wasn't like the guy didn't have a life other than me—shocking, to say the least.

But contrary to what some people believed, I did know how to trust my gut, even though it was sometimes a little on the late side. It was that twisty feeling that made me call Archer again. Considering I was supposed to leave in about a week and a half, him not answering my calls wasn't a good sign.

"Hey, man. Sorry, things have been crazy," Archer said instead of hello.

I breathed out a sigh of relief. Like I'd thought, he'd been busy, but now he was going to tell me all the ways this whole thing was going to fucking kill it.

"No worries. I just wanted to touch base and see if there's anything I need to do. There's not that much time and—"

"Hey, listen, before you go any further, I have some bad news…"

My gut dropped, and I began pacing Marcus's bedroom.

"I don't think it's going to work out…and by *I don't*

think, I mean it's not. Nothing personal, Kai, but my business partner wants to go another direction."

"Business partner?" We'd been talking about this for how long, and this was the first time I was hearing about a business partner.

"Yeah, a friend of mine. I didn't mention him? Anyway, I talked to him about you, but he said he's not interested. He wants someone who's a sure thing."

"I'm a sure thing! You never said this was something you had to run by another person. As far as I knew, this was one hundred percent going down. What the fuck, Archer? I already gave my notice at Driftwood. My boss has started interviewing people. You said I'd have an apartment there too!"

"Tell your boss you want to stay. I was just trying to help you out, but some shit fell through. That's not my fault. You can't depend on everyone else to take care of your stuff for you."

You can't depend on everyone else to take care of your stuff for you…

That's what I was trying *not* to do.

"*You* called *me*!" I yelled, heart in my throat and bile burning my esophagus. But the thing was, Archer was right. I never should have depended on him or anyone else. I was so fucking stupid to trust some guy I used to hang out with, rearranging my whole life without any guarantee or contract. At twenty-six years old, I should have known better.

"I'm sorry, Kai, but I gotta go. We'll talk soon, and if anything changes, I'll let you know!"

And then, without another word, Archer ended the call.

Stunned, I walked out to the balcony and fell down onto the futon. But once the initial shock wore off, it morphed into something that felt even worse—embarrassment and feeling like a failure. I'd just recently told my family. They'd supported me and believed in me, and now I was supposed to tell them that nope, I still didn't have my shit together.

I truly thought I would make that bar something special, that I'd be good at it. That Marcus would come see me in Atlanta, and while I knew I'd never have what he did, I'd have *something*—something I helped build.

But now I had to tell him that his boyfriend was a loser…and, oh hey, could I stay with him longer? Assuming I could keep my job, which meant I'd have to go crawling back to Declan too. If he hadn't hired anyone, I knew he would keep me, but he shouldn't have to.

And all that made me think of Marcus again. I wanted to be with him. I didn't want him to have to take care of me, and I knew he would feel like he did. I wasn't sure how to handle that.

★ ★ ★

I CALLED IN at work, which made me feel even more like shit, but I knew I couldn't be there. I just wanted Marcus, which was scary and confusing, especially since I felt bad needing him, putting my shit on his plate this way.

I'd just gotten out of the shower and was curled up on the couch, wearing one of his T-shirts and a pair of underwear, when I heard the lock and the door opening. He wouldn't be able to see me because the back of the couch was between us, but he would have seen my car in the driveway.

"Kai?" he called out, his voice like a warm blanket around me.

"Over here." I sat up, fought to bury all those poor-me feelings that I really fucking hated and tried not to ever let myself feel.

Marcus had an open house today. He didn't always go to those himself, but it was an important client and a very expensive house, so he'd wanted to handle it himself. He wore a pair of slacks and a white button-up with the sleeves rolled up to his elbows. It was maybe the hottest look in existence, and all men should be forced to wear it.

"Are you sick?" He brushed the back of his hand against my forehead, which was such a caretaker thing and totally Marcus.

"No, but I want you." I pushed up onto my knees and started unbuttoning his shirt. I wanted him to fuck me before I told him that his boyfriend was an immature slacker who could be out of a job soon.

Marcus frowned. "Not that you don't look fine as fuck in my shirt, and I would die to get inside your ass, but what's wrong?" He held my wrists, trying to stop me from finishing with his buttons.

"Nothing. I want to have sex with my boyfriend." I stood up on the cushions and wrapped my arms around his shoulders, pressing my lips to his.

Marcus growled in return, holding my ass as I tangled my legs around his waist. He lifted me, walked around the couch, and sat down with me on his lap. When I tried to kiss him again, he pulled back. "What's wrong, baby boy?"

I want to be good enough for you. I want to prove I want you and maybe need you, but because I love you and not for what you can do for me.

"I'll tell you afterward, I promise, but right now my hole is really hungry for your cock." I scooted back some, palming his thick erection and making him hiss. The look he gave me was conflicted, part desire and part worry, which just made me love him more. "Please, baby."

Marcus's stare turned smoldering, like he was fighting it

but couldn't contain his need for me, which I was still trying to wrap my head around.

He shoved his large hand down the back of my underwear, fingers sliding along my crease. "I'll feed your hungry little hole, but afterward I won't let you up until you talk to me."

I grinned because how could I not? He was fucking incredible, and I was so damn lucky to have him. Why, out of all the men he could have, Marcus chose me still blew my mind.

His lips crashed down on mine, the last rein he had on his control finally snapping.

We kissed like we were starving for each other, like we couldn't breathe unless our lips were attached.

Marcus pulled back just enough to rip my shirt over my head, and then his mouth possessed mine again. I worked the rest of the buttons on his shirt while his tongue ravaged me, my balls already so full, I could come any second.

His mouth trailed wet kisses down my neck, my chest, until he reached my pierced nipple, which he sucked, then dug into with his teeth. Sharp pain stung my pec before melting into pleasure, and my hand at the back of his head pulled him closer.

"Do you like that?" he asked. "Like it when I bite and suck on you?"

"Yes, fuck yes." I liked everything he did to me.

Marcus did it again and again, marking me up, alternating between the suction of his mouth and the pressure of his teeth.

When I fought to tug his shirt off, Marcus leaned forward to make it easier. I lifted his arm, nuzzled his pit, and savored the scent and taste of soap and salt on his skin. Marcus moaned in response, and when I pulled back, his intense stare was a promise of all the pleasure he would give me. And I needed to give it to him too.

"Don't move," I said, earning one of his famous cocked brows.

"Since when are you in charge here?"

"Please don't move," I asked because this was one of the only places I wanted Marcus to be a little bossy.

"For now," he replied.

"Always making things difficult," I teased.

"I wouldn't be me if I didn't."

No, he wouldn't. And I wouldn't love him as much either.

I slid to the floor, kissing the beautiful brown skin of his torso as I went. When I got to my knees, I pulled his pants off, then nuzzled his thick bulge, licked and sucked him through the fabric of his underwear, breathed in the heady scent of musk and desire clinging to Marcus's skin.

"Jesus, I love this dick," I said, rubbing my face against it like I was trying to get his smell all over me. *I love you.*

"It loves you too. Why don't you take it out so I can show you how much?"

"Because I want to show *you*."

Still, I did remove his underwear, watching Marcus's hard and heavy length flex against his belly. Looking up at him, I kissed his balls—one, then the other—our gazes never disengaging.

"Fuck, baby boy. Kiss my cock. I know you wanna worship it. You gotta be real good if you want me in that tight hole of yours."

Shivers started at my nape and raced down my spine. "Like this?" I asked, pressing my lips to the base of his thick shaft.

"Fuck yes. Now go all the way up, and then I want you to

suck on the head. You're not allowed to look away, though. Keep those pretty brown eyes on me so you can see how much I want you."

I'd never needed to be wanted more than I did by Marcus.

"Such a Daddy," I joked before leaning down, looking at him as I pressed kisses up his shaft.

His stare hypnotized me, made me feel things deep inside. No one had ever looked at me the way Marcus did. I didn't know if it meant he felt as strongly for me as I did for him, but I wasn't dumb enough not to realize I was something special to him. That much was clear in the way he treated me. It made me want to be even better for him, to prove myself worthy of him.

Marcus hissed when I reached his crown and sucked on the head the way he'd told me to. His pupils were so wide, almost none of the color showed in them.

My own dick throbbed. I wanted relief, to get swept up into an orgasm, but just as much, I wanted this to last.

"Fuck, baby boy, look at you down there on your knees for me. It's the sexiest thing I've ever seen. You'd sit there all night if I asked you to, wouldn't you, just sucking on my cock because you know it's what I want."

"Fuck yes," I admitted before circling his dick with my tongue, then easing it into my mouth again.

His body was hot against mine, his scent clean but tinged with natural musk.

"Lower your mouth, but keep those eyes on me."

I did as Marcus said, bobbing my head on his thick erection as we watched each other with careful expressions in our eyes. Was he hiding something too?

"Jesus, get up here." He grabbed my arms and tugged me into his lap so I was straddling him again.

A bottle of lube and a condom sat on the table beside us.

Marcus raised his brow as if to say, *Planned this, huh?* which made me grin. "I know what I want," I told him, "and when I want it, I don't like to wait."

"You still always causing trouble."

"You like that about me. You like that I shake up your carefully constructed world."

Something changed in Marcus's gaze, like he was trying to shut down more but couldn't. His gaze softened and pulled me in deeper, and then his hand wrapped around the back of my head, tugging me close, his tongue plunging into my mouth.

We made out while Marcus grabbed the bottle, opened it, and lubed his fingers. He held my ass, his fingers dipping between my cheeks before a slick digit rubbed my rim.

"Fuck yes," I said into his mouth, rotating my hips so our cocks rubbed together. "Get your dick inside me, baby."

"You don't get to make the rules tonight," he reminded me, taking possession of my mouth again. At the same time, he did push his finger inside me, slowly working it in and out of my hole.

One became two, and I was riding his digits while he played with my pierced nipples again, licking and nibbling, sucking and blowing on them, which made goose bumps cover my skin.

"Marcus…God…I need you so much. I had such a shitty day, and I just wanted you…knew you'd make it better." And he did, probably more than he should have.

"Christ, you're gonna fucking wreck me. I need inside you." He reached for the condom, but I placed a hand on his wrist.

"Do we need it? If you'd feel more comfortable suited up, that's fine, but I'm tested regularly. I went in right before I moved in here, and I haven't been with anyone but you…and

I've never...without a rubber."

I swear his whole fucking body vibrated, like any second his skin would crack and he would burst free of it. I wasn't sure if that was a good thing until he said, "You're gonna let me shoot my load in your tight little hole? Gonna let me fill you up and watch it leak out of you?"

"Holy shit. Don't say stuff like that unless you want me to come before this even begins."

Marcus chuckled, and I did too. "I'm negative too. I've been tested recently, and I don't fuck without protection either." And PrEP was also part of each of our daily routines.

"We don't have to. I—"

"I want to," he admitted. "Now lube up my cock and ride it for me."

I trembled in response, pleasure skating down my spine and landing in my groin. "You're the worst. Stop making me want you so much," I said as I slicked up my hand, then wrapped it around Marcus's dick.

"This is on me, huh? You're the one who kept flirting, and look at us now. This is all your fault."

"Yeah, but are you complaining?"

His voice turned serious when he said, "No."

Jesus, Marcus Alston was going to be the death of me.

I pushed up onto my knees, holding the base of his cock as I maneuvered it so I could slowly lower myself. He'd opened my hole up good with his fingers, but it was still uncomfortable at first, the way it always was, my body accepting something inside.

"That's it, baby boy. Take me. You know you want it, want my cock. That ass was made for me, wasn't it? Tell me your ass was made for me."

There was nothing in the world hotter than Marcus dirty-talking. His mouth was a national damn treasure of filth that I fucking loved. "My ass was made for you...but doesn't that mean your cock was made for me?"

I lowered myself more, the pressure and stretch so damn welcome. Before I knew it, he was buried to the hilt, me sitting on his lap with my favorite dick wedged inside me.

"Ride me," he said instead of answering, and I did, raising and lowering myself on his thick shaft. It hit me just right, made pleasure explode through every inch of my body.

I dropped my head back, but he tugged it forward again, Marcus's mouth and tongue on my lips before he licked my piercings, playing with them, fingers digging into my ass cheeks.

He lowered himself on the couch some to make it easier, leaned back, and ran a hand down my torso. "That's it, baby boy. Show me how well you can take that dick. Ride it until I empty my balls, filling you up with my load. Let's see if you can come hands-free, shoot all over my chest with just my dick in your ass. Can you do it? You can rub your cum into my skin and make me smell like you."

"Oh fuck." My thighs began to tremble, my whole body tingling, a steady feeling that just increased each time I rose and sat on Marcus's dick. Even more than that, it was what he said, his words fucking my brain the same way his dick did my ass, and there was nothing sexier than when your head was completely into the sex like this.

"That's it, take my cock in your hungry hole. Milk a load out of my balls, Kai. My cum is all yours."

Something about those words did me in, made my nuts tighten, dizziness sweeping through me as I splintered apart, spurting my release all over my stomach and Marcus's, my cum running down his groin and into the dark curls there. It was like I couldn't stop; each time I lowered myself on him, his dick hitting my prostate, I shot again, and then it was his cock twitching, spurting, Marcus's load just where it belonged—inside me.

Chapter Twenty-Seven
Marcus

I PULLED KAI'S head toward me again, needing to kiss him once more. It was slow, sensual, my tongue easing into his mouth like we had the rest of our lives to do this, but I had a feeling whatever he was going to say, I wouldn't like it. That for the first time in my life, I had a boyfriend and I wanted more, and he was likely going to tell me this was over.

When I pulled back, I took his hand and rubbed his load into my skin. Kai sucked in a sharp breath like the action surprised him, but he let me do it before I gently turned us so we were lying down, with him on top of me.

"We're gonna get cum and sweat on your couch."

"I don't give a shit. I'll clean it. What's wrong? Just tell me." I was on my back, his stomach and chest against mine. I held his ass, then dipped my fingers lower so I could play with his puffy, swollen hole that was slick with my cum.

"Ugh. I'm an idiot, and I don't want to tell you. It's embarrassing." He buried his face in my neck, and I frowned. It was embarrassing? Maybe this wasn't what I thought it would be.

"You've met my friends. You have nothing to worry about." Kai chuckled the way I'd hoped he would but then stiffened. He tried to get up, but I held him down. "If you really want to get free, all you have to do is ask, but if you don't use the words, I'm taking that as permission to hold you where I want you to be."

He rolled his eyes. "Of course you have to go and be fair." He sighed. "I'm not going to Atlanta. It was…fuck, it was probably never going to happen, and I'm the flaky idiot who trusts everyone and just believed what Archer said."

This time it was my turn to stiffen. I swatted his ass. "Don't talk about my boyfriend that way."

"Why are you the sweetest man in the world?"

I looked away from him. "I'm not. Fuck Archer. Whatever happened, that's on him, not you. It's not your fault he lied or misled you or whatever it was."

"But you asked me about contracts, and I didn't push for them. I just listened to everything he said and rearranged my whole fucking life around it. What if Declan has already replaced me?"

"He won't. If you want your job back, it's yours."

Kai shook his head. "You can't make Declan keep me. How would that be fair to the other person? He's already been interviewing. And…that's the thing. You can't fix everything for me. I know it comes from the heart, but this whole situation proves I'm a mess and need to learn how to make better decisions."

This time when Kai tried to sit up, I let him.

"How am I supposed to tell my family I fucked up? They're going to feel sorry for me and again want me to move home. My other choice is to keep living here with you when I don't even know if I have a job and—"

"Is that so bad?"

"Yes!" Kai shouted, then sighed. "Shit. Not the way that sounded. I love being here with you, Marcus. I just… I don't have anything to offer you. I can't give you the things you can give me and…what? You're going to help support me for the rest of my life? Take me to meet your parents, your bartender boyfriend who everyone thinks is a little too much?"

"Fuck everyone." Didn't he see that *I* didn't think he was too much? That it had taken Kai to make me want to belong to someone else? "And you."

He crossed his arms. "Fuck me?"

"You said you don't have anything to offer me. You, Kai. What makes you think I need someone who can buy me shit? Or who has what you seem to think of as a more worthy career than bartending? I don't give a damn about that stuff."

"Because you have things! What happens if you resent me?"

I sighed. "That's possible in any relationship. It's not what people want to think about, but it's real. A large percentage of relationships fail. People resent each other. People fight. I don't know the first thing about being someone's boyfriend, but I'm here, Kai. You're the one running. You're the one using the kind of excuses I usually would. I grew up in a house where people could buy me shit and give me everything I wanted in that way. That's not what I'm looking for in a relationship. You have nothing to prove to me."

The expression on his face turned contemplative, his brows pulled together as he looked at me. I'd basically spilled my guts to him in a way I never had with anyone else, and it was killing me not to get up and walk away, to pretend it didn't matter and that I didn't care about him because it was so much fucking safer that way. But the truth was, I wanted him, and I wasn't sure there was anything I wouldn't do to have him.

"Oh…that makes sense. I never thought about it that way. I just want to be good for you."

"You are," I said, pulling him close. Kai came easily, straddling my lap.

"But I want to be good for me too. I want something that's mine. I don't know why I didn't care about that until recently. It's not that I don't think bartending is a valid career. I want to love what I do, and I want to know that I can make it on my own if I need to. But how does that happen if I don't even know the answer to those questions?"

I nodded because I could understand that. I would be the same way. Helping was easy for me and I wanted to do it, but I got his need for independence, even if I thought sometimes you had to get help to give you the independence you needed. It was why I'd helped Dec with Driftwood and Parker with Beach Buns, and now they were doing it on their own. "Okay…so what do you need from me, baby boy? For me to step back?"

"No. God no. Maybe I should, but I'm too selfish. Plus, you just marked your territory *inside* me, so I'm basically yours for however long you want me."

Wasn't it some shit that I wanted to open my mouth and tell him I wanted him forever? "Then we'll figure it out. If you want to go home, you can, but I think you should stay here and talk to Dec about the job."

"That's going to be a fun conversation. How fucking embarrassing."

"I can—" He gave me a look, and I chuckled. "Okay, have fun with it, then. But if you need my help, I'm here. Declan will understand. He loves you and doesn't want to lose you at Driftwood. The rest, we'll handle together."

Kai nodded, but I could tell he was unsure how he felt. And while I was happy he was staying, it didn't change the fact that I knew he didn't want to. That he hadn't chosen to be here, hadn't chosen me. It was just the hand he'd been dealt. It probably made me an asshole that I was glad he wasn't moving to Atlanta.

"Thank you for liking me the way I am and for always being real with me. That means more to me than you'll ever know."

But I wasn't real with him, not truly. If I were, my ass would have admitted I loved him and had considered locking him in my room to keep him here or following him to Atlanta. That since the last *Vers* recording, all I'd thought about and hoped was that he'd ask me to go with him.

"Well, you did let me breed you, so that was a good thank-you," I teased. "Are you going to keep letting me fill your hole with my cum?"

"Yes. God yes. I can feel it inside me, and I'm totally wondering when we can do it again…but I should also put some underwear on, and we should consider getting a new couch."

I laughed just as my stomach growled.

"Let me feed you." Kai stood and tugged his trunks on.

"You don't have to do that."

"I know. I want to."

He headed for the kitchen, and something clicked in my head. I didn't know what took me so long to see it. I stood and followed him. "You like cooking."

"Yep. Are you just figuring that out?" he joked.

"Maybe that's your answer, and it's been staring us in the face the whole time."

I saw his eyes light up, saw the glimmer there that brightened by the second, and damn if it wasn't one of the most beautiful things I'd ever seen.

"Culinary school?"

I shrugged. "Why not?"

I could see him working through it, see the wheels turning in Kai's brain. He was thinking about this. He was seriously considering it. And when he smiled, I knew something had clicked for him as well.

"How, though? It would be expensive...but I could get loans. Between work, bills, and life... Oh my God. Do you think I can do this? Do I want to?" He paused a moment. "Holy shit. I want this. Jesus, Marcus. How in the hell did we not think of this earlier? I love feeding people."

His excitement was infectious. I felt it rolling off him, seeping into my skin.

"I don't want to get my hopes up too much." He looked at me, his eyes glittering with unshed tears. "But I want to do this. I want to do this in ways I've never wanted anything else. Atlanta was just because I had to do something. This..." This was important in a different way. It was something he really desired. Kai wrapped his arms around me like it had been me who'd given him something. "I don't even know if I can make this happen, but thank you. I don't know what I would do without you."

I'd lived my whole life not needing anyone except *The Vers* crew and knowing they were the only ones who needed me, but Kai had changed everything. I didn't know what I would do without him either, and I hoped like hell I would never find out. I'd always prided myself on keeping it real, but this? Love? It was the realest thing of all, and I hadn't known it until Kai.

"You're the one who's going to have to do the work." I patted his ass.

"Don't do that. Don't pretend you didn't have a hand in it. You help everyone, Marcus. You make all our lives better. I'm gonna spend my days making sure you know that."

I nodded because I wasn't in the mood to argue, and I knew he wouldn't let it go. "Let's make some food, and then I'm gonna take you to bed and breed your hole again."

Kai smiled. "Best. Night. Ever."

Damned if I didn't agree.

Chapter Twenty-Eight
Kai

I WENT TO talk to Declan before speaking to my family. I'd called him earlier, when I knew he would be at Driftwood doing his monthly accounting, and asked if I could come in and have a conversation with him. Declan agreed, which I knew he would.

I waved at Andy, who was bartending when I got there.

"You're leaving soon, right, Kai? It's gonna suck to see you go."

Little did he know, I wouldn't be leaving and would hopefully still have a job at Driftwood. "We'll see what happens," I replied because it was the only response I could think of. Andy frowned, clearly confused, but I just continued toward Declan's office.

I knocked even though the door wasn't completely closed. It slid open a bit more, and Declan looked up, his hair messy like he'd run his hand through it too many times to count.

"Hey, Kai. Come in."

"Hey, handsome." I sat in the chair across from him.

"Still a flirt, I see," he joked.

"You expected it to change since my last shift?" I tossed back, then sobered. "Listen…I'm just going to spit it out because this is embarrassing enough. The Atlanta job is not happening. Archer didn't really care about me working for him, and so I was wondering if—"

"Yes."

"I didn't ask anything yet."

"If you're asking if you can stay, then yes. I haven't hired anyone. I don't like change...or most people...and for whatever reason I haven't figured out yet, I like you, so yes."

I frowned. "Did Marcus call and tell you?"

Declan's forehead wrinkled. "Why would Marcus do that? Okay, well, he would, but not if you didn't want him to, which it sounds like you didn't."

He was right. Marcus wouldn't go back on his word to me. "I know. Sorry. I just..." My head tilted down. I tried to stop the words from coming out because all they did was add even more shame, but I couldn't seem to keep them at bay. "I want to be good enough for him. I want him to know I'm with him because it's where I want to be, not because I need him or don't have another option."

"Marcus is crazy about you. None of us have ever seen him like this."

"That doesn't change the fact that I'm a lot...and that he has so much more to offer than I do. If I can't stand on my own, what if there comes a point where Marcus thinks I only care about what he can give me? What if he gets tired of putting up with me?"

"Umm...I'm not the best with stuff like this, but Marcus wouldn't think that. He cares about you, and Marcus likes to be there for people he cares about."

"I want to be there for him just as much."

"You are. It doesn't have to be monetarily. There are lots of ways to be there for someone, Kai, and whatever you do for Marcus, it's good for him and he appreciates it. Maybe there are some things you give Marcus that no one else can, and it has nothing to do with what you decide to do with your life."

It was on the tip of my tongue to make a joke about sex, but this didn't feel like a joking matter.

Declan saved me from having to respond by adding, "I'm sorry things didn't work out with Atlanta, but I can't act like I'm not happy you'll still be here. It would have been strange if Marcus had moved away."

My gaze snapped to him. "Marcus was thinking about going?" My pulse thudded a rapid beat against my skin. He would have done that for me? Left everything behind?

"Oh fuck. Let's pretend I didn't say that. Can't wait to see you back at work!"

But I couldn't forget. I also knew that Declan wouldn't give me any more information. Still, it was all I thought about while we talked about my schedule and how I was going to look into going to culinary school. That I wasn't sure where I would end up, and if I could make it work in LA county, that I might need to change my hours. And if it all got too expensive, that I'd have to move back to Riverside.

Declan was agreeable to everything. Damn, I was lucky to have him in my life. I was lucky to have them all in my life.

Especially Marcus.

★ ★ ★

"FUCK ARCHER," MOM said, which didn't surprise me in the least. "He doesn't know what he's missing, passing up on my son. I never liked him."

Yeah, well, apparently, he didn't like me much either. "I guess it wasn't meant to be. I just hate that it wasn't on my terms." I waved my hand. "I don't want to talk about that, though. After I told Marcus last night, I was going to make us something to eat, and he mentioned culinary school. You know how much I love to feed people, and it just... I can't explain it. Everything clicked into place, and I realized this was it. This is what I'm supposed to do." The thought of making a career out of cooking for people fit into my life the same way Marcus had, like there had always been a place cut out just for him, only I didn't know it until he filled it.

"I think that's a damn good idea. You've always loved feeding people. It's perfect, actually."

"Yeah, I think so too. I don't know how much it'll be, but I'm hoping I can make it work. Marcus said I can stay with him. He even offered to help, but I don't want him to have to do that."

She looked at me in that way moms did that told me she thought I was being an idiot.

"What?" I asked.

"Don't be stubborn, Kai. I'm not saying don't work hard and handle your business. I respect the hell out of you for wanting to be your own man. But don't bite off your nose to spite your face either. Don't be so full of pride that all you do is end up hurting yourself and those you love."

"I'm not doing that."

"Part of lovin' folks is being there when they need you. Part of that is also being willing to let them in and to lean on each other when you need it. Do you think there haven't been times in our lives when I gave more than Dad in some ways or he gave more than me? There are things he can do for me that I could never do for him, but he comes to me for certain things too. That's what a relationship is. You and Marcus just need to find your balance."

"I'm in love with him," I admitted.

"I knew that the second I saw you with him. That man loves you too."

He'd never told me, but I wanted that, so fucking much. "Declan said he was considering moving to Atlanta with me. I had no idea."

"Sounds like the two of you need to talk."

"Yeah, well, that's too easy," I joked, but then, "Do you really think someone like him could love someone like me?"

Mama reached over and grabbed my hand. "What do you mean, someone like you? Someone kind, smart, funny, handsome, and who likes to protect and take care of those he loves? Yeah, I think he could love someone like that. Being an adult means getting your hands messy sometimes, and that's what you need to do. Talk to him. Tell him how you feel. Make decisions together. If you're old enough to love someone, you're old enough to act like it. If that man was willing to leave everything behind for you, what are you willing to do for him? At least be willing to tell him how you feel. And the rest, you sit down and figure out together."

She was right. Moms usually were. I damn sure knew I wanted Marcus, and I would do whatever I could to have him.

"We should look into some schools," Mom said, and I agreed. Marcus was supposed to have dinner with his folks later, so I had hours to kill before he got home. "In the Santa Monica area. I love you and you're always welcome home, but you belong with Marcus."

I wanted to belong with him. I wanted to be with him.

We sat at the computer together and looked things up. I made a few appointments with admissions offices to get more information, made a list of costs, wrote down pros and cons of each place.

"I should probably head out." I stood and stretched. Dad was home now. He hadn't hidden his excitement over this new turn of events. He joked about Marcus and me inviting them over to our place for some food. I liked the sound of that—*our* place. I wanted to share everything I could with Marcus.

I smiled when my cell rang, assuming it was him. If his parents fucked up tonight and bailed on him, I would lose my shit. Marcus deserved so much better. He deserved to be wanted. He knew how much I needed him, right?

When I tugged my phone from my pocket and saw Declan's name, I frowned. It was possible he was calling because he needed me at work, but the immediate twist in my gut said it was something else.

Still, I tried to ignore the warning in my stomach and answered with, "Hey, handsome."

"Everything is okay, so don't stress—"

"What the fuck. If you start with that, shit isn't okay. What happened?" Mom and Dad both watched me, Mom coming closer and placing her hand on my arm in support. It didn't stop my heart from trying to beat out of my chest or the dizziness that swept through me.

"Marcus got into a car accident on the ten. He's okay, but he did break an arm and he's going to need surgery on it. We're at UCLA Santa Monica. His phone got busted, but they had Corbin listed as his emergency contact from a previous procedure."

"I'm in Riverside. I'll be there as fast as I can. Tell him…" *Tell him I love him. Tell him I'm sorry I let dumb shit matter.* "Just tell him I'm on my way." Everything else needed to be said in person.

Chapter Twenty-Nine
Marcus

"THIS FUCKING SUCKS," I grumbled, sitting in the hospital bed at the UCLA Santa Monica ortho center. They couldn't do the surgery on my busted arm for a few days, but they wanted to keep me overnight because they were worried about a head injury, which was frustrating because I was fine. "I have too much shit going on at work to take time off."

"Maybe don't be a workaholic when you just got into a car accident," Corbin said.

"If people didn't drive like idiots, I wouldn't have gotten in a car accident." I tugged on the annoying sling digging into my neck. Was I supposed to wear this for an extended period of time? If so, that shit wasn't happening.

"Yes, well, there's no going back in time to change that, so you need to listen to the doctors and stop being a brat," Parker said.

"Do you know me?" I asked in unison with Declan's, "Do you know him?"

The three of them laughed, but I was too pissed and grumpy to do that. My parents had flaked on dinner, and then I'd gotten into a wreck. Not that the accident was their fault, but it was something else weighing on me.

Not only that, but...but I wanted Kai to be here, and I

hated needing someone that way. It was one thing with Corbin, Parker, and Declan, but now my heart was bigger, easier to bruise and batter, because all he'd done was make the thing grow and feel more vulnerable.

"Excuse me. There are already three people back there," I heard from the hallway.

"That's my son's boyfriend in that room!"

My gaze snapped toward the doorway just as Kai came bursting into the room. His pupils were blown wide, his expression panicked. The second he saw me, his eyes welled with tears.

"Hey, come here. I'm okay," I said, feeling that stupid organ in my chest swell even more.

"Oh God. Even now you're trying to console me. I should be consoling you."

Bernard stepped up behind him, then Ann, Jalen, and Faith. They were all here. They'd all come for me? For a stupid broken arm and a bruised head?

"Come here, baby boy," I said again, not sure what other words to even use at that moment. There was too much feeling to choose anything else to settle on. I was afraid of what would come out if I tried.

"There are too many people in this room," the nurse reiterated. "We're going to need some of you to step out."

Kai took one step toward me, then another, ignoring her. My gaze was glued on him as he said, "I'm in love with you...and I choose you... I don't know if you wondered if I didn't, if you thought I was here simply because everything else fell through, but I'm with you because I love you and I would always choose you. I might not have known it before, but I know it now, and...I'm in love with you. I said that. At least once. Maybe twice, but...surprise?" He grinned, tears streaming down his face now.

"Oh, wow," the nurse said.

"Aww. What the fuck. That's the cutest thing ever," Corbin added. "Tell him you love him too, Marcus."

"Shut up, Corbin," Parker and Declan said. Something about his words unstuck the truth that had been trapped in my chest.

"I love you too, Kai."

"My baby is in love," Ann said, but I couldn't focus on anyone but Kai as he closed the distance between us and climbed right onto the bed with me. He straddled my legs but didn't put his weight on me.

"Um…" I heard in the background, likely from the nurse.

"Can you pretend you didn't see that? We'll leave and…you know, give them some privacy. They'll be good, I promise. How has your shift been going?" Corbin charmed her as I heard the room emptying out, the door closing with a soft *click*.

"You're hurt," Kai said.

"It's just a broken arm." I cupped his face with my good hand.

"I need you," he blurted. "I didn't want to need you in some ways because I knew in here, I did." He touched his chest. "But I need you and I'm in love with you. I would pick you over Atlanta, culinary school, anything else, Marcus. I don't care if that's too much or if it's irresponsible, and I know you; there are all sorts of things going on inside your head about love and life and everything else, but I'm listening to my heart, and I know you really want to as well. There are so many things you do for me, and I don't want to be a burden, but I know I can take care of you too. We can take care of each other."

I smiled. "Do I get to speak now?"

"Only if you say something I wanna hear."

I grinned because how could I not? "You take care of me now, Kai. You have from the start. No one makes me feel the way you do." I thought about the time he'd asked me if my house, if all the things I had, was enough. "Nothing but having you will ever be enough for me."

He leaned close, kissed the bruise on my lip, then the other corner of my mouth. "Jesus, Marcus. I love you. You thought about going to Atlanta for me?"

I growled. "I hate my friends."

"No you don't…and you love me."

"I do."

Kai kissed my neck, and I leaned back to give him better access. "I'm going to take such good care of you while you're hurt…won't let you work at all. I hope you know that."

"I changed my mind."

Kai chuckled. "No takebacks. You're stuck with me."

"No," I replied. "I choose you."

Kai leaned back, looked at me, and smiled. "We're so fucking cute."

And that didn't even bother me the way it should.

Eventually, he climbed off me. His family came back in first, his mom fussing over me and everyone treating me like I belonged. They didn't stay long, but they didn't need to. I was just honored they had come, that they knew Kai loved me, which made me important to them.

When the guys came back in, Sebastian and Elliott were there too. Apparently, when Sebastian Cole was around, they let you do whatever you wanted, and there were no complaints about the number of people in the room.

Kai sat on the edge of the bed, holding my hand while we all chatted—all of them not only loving me, but showing me, making me feel it, and that meant more to me than I could ever say.

"Do your parents know you're here?" Declan asked.

"I didn't call them."

"Shit. I didn't either. I didn't have their number. I should do that now."

I shook my head at Dec. "Nah, it's fine. I'll do it tomorrow."

"Are you sure?" Kai asked, and I nodded.

For now, everything was perfect.

★ ★ ★

"I HATE THIS. Where's my laptop? We need to get me a new cell phone," I grumbled at Kai the next day.

"We've literally been home for thirty-five minutes. You'll survive."

"You hid my laptop!"

"You did the same with Corbin's phone once."

"That was different." I pushed up from the couch and went to look at the fish tank. It was calming, and I needed that. I had no idea what to do with myself. I had surgery scheduled in two days. I was in pain, my car was totaled, and…oh. I smiled when Kai wrapped his arms around me from behind, then slid a hand down my sweats to grab my cock.

This was nice. This made everything better.

"Do you want me to give you a blowjob? Will that help?"

"The answer to that question will always be yes."

So he blew me, then fixed me lunch. I complained from the couch, but that was how I rolled, and he told me I was being an idiot because that was how he rolled, and it was actually fucking awesome in a way that had much more to do with my heart than my head.

I had soup because I needed to eat light things, and then

Kai gave me a pain pill. Before I took a nap, I used his phone to send an email to my parents because he wouldn't even let me have my laptop for that. I told myself I should call or at least text, but I just felt too good and I didn't want to risk being brought down.

Before I knew it, I was curled up on the couch, the fuzzy edges of my consciousness drifting further away.

I didn't know how much time had passed when I heard Kai's muffled voice in the background.

"He can stay with us after surgery," my mom said.

"No. He'll want to be home. I'll be here with him. I got time off work," Kai told her.

"Are you and my son in a relationship?" Dad asked. I knew I should speak up, that I should let them know I was awake, but for whatever reason, I didn't.

"Yes. I'm in love with him. I know I might not be what you want for your son, but—"

"I want someone who is good for him," Mom interrupted. "Someone who understands him and makes him happy. Is that you?"

"Yes," Kai replied. "There's nothing I wouldn't do for him, and he knows that." I was just about to speak up, to tell them Kai was right and how much he meant to me, when Kai spoke again. "Can he say the same about you?"

"Excuse me?" Dad said, and…holy shit. People didn't speak to my parents the way Kai just had. Even I didn't.

"I'm not trying to be hurtful, and in a lot of ways it's not my business, but on the other hand…it's Marcus, and Marcus is my man and my business, and he deserves better, Mr. and Mrs. Alston."

My heart thudded against my chest, throbbed and echoed through my whole body, hearing Kai have my back this way.

"My son knows we love him," Mom bristled, but I could

hear the insecurity in her voice.

"Yes, he does, but that doesn't mean he doesn't deserve more. He should know he comes first. I didn't give him that in the beginning either, and I damn sure plan not to make that mistake again."

I couldn't keep quiet anymore, so I sat up. "Kai?"

He rushed over. "Hey, baby. How are you feeling?" He knelt in front of me, worry in his gaze like I had more than a broken arm, and this right here, him, was what love felt like.

"I'm fine." I leaned in and kissed his forehead. Mom and Dad walked over and around the couch so they were in front of us.

"Oh, Marcus," Mom said, the tone of her voice softer than I'd ever heard it. "We really made a mess of things, didn't we?"

I wasn't sure how to respond to that, my gaze darting back and forth between my parents. I could see the concern in both their faces, mixed with confusion because the truth was, the three of us were just built differently. I didn't think they needed the same things I did when it came to love. That didn't make them bad people, and hell, if it hadn't been for the Beach Bums coming into my life all those years ago, and then Kai, maybe I wouldn't have needed more either, but I did.

"I know you love me," I told them as Kai sat beside me on the couch. "I just…"

"We haven't done the best job of showing you," Dad said. "And I'm sorry about that. Alston Architecture was our dream. We worked so hard for it, put everything into it, and we didn't make sure you knew you were the dream we hadn't known we had."

My brows pinched together because that… Fuck, I'd never heard my dad speak that way in my life.

Mom spoke next. "In my head, building Alston became about you, giving this empire to you because we loved you so much, but I know I'm not the best in showing it in other ways. But please don't ever doubt what you mean to us. Your dad and I, we love each other in our own way, and it's important for us to remember that it isn't enough for everyone. I'm not perfect. I—"

"I'm sure as shit not perfect either, Mom. I don't expect that. I just want to make plans with you and know they aren't going to get canceled more often than not because something came up at work." I thought about how I'd been upset I didn't have my laptop earlier, and the many times I'd chosen work over spending time with my friends. "And I know I need to be better about that myself." I put a hand on Kai's thigh. "Because this? The people you love? They're the most important thing."

My mom nodded, letting a single tear leak free. "They are. You scared the life out of me, Marcus, and when I realized my son sent me an *email* to tell me he got in a car accident... That was a wake-up call."

"For me too, son," Dad said.

When my parents came closer, I stood, the two of them wrapping me into their arms, and I had to admit, I was kinda seeing why Corbin enjoyed hugs so much.

I didn't know if anything would change, but for now, I had hope, and I knew that regardless of how things went with my family, I had Kai, Elliott, Sebastian, and the Beach Bums. That would always be enough for me.

Epilogue

Kai

December

"I LOOK GOOD. Don't I look good?" Corbin asked, running his hand down his tux.

"You look great, cutie." I winked at him. We were all at a fundraiser Elliott's mom, Cat, had organized for World AIDS Day. While there had been so many incredible strides and those who were positive living long and healthy lives, there was still more that could be done. She was raising money for research and education.

"I love your boyfriend," Corbin told Marcus, who chuckled in response.

I lived with Marcus, of course, because now that I had him, I sure as shit didn't want to be away from him. We'd come to an agreement about money and school. I'd applied for loans, but what I couldn't get covered, I was going to let Marcus help with. It came from love, and I'd let myself accept that it was okay to lean on him some. We were in love, and relationships were about give and take. I'd told him I wanted to pay him back, and Marcus had agreed without arguing, but I also knew he wouldn't want to take it. We'd cross that bridge in a million years when I actually had money. Whatever we decided, I knew it wouldn't come between us.

"He's an annoying little shit," Declan said, smiling before

he took a drink of his champagne.

"Come on, handsome. Don't pretend I'm not your favorite," I joked back.

"He has a point," Sebastian added playfully.

"Traitor," Declan countered. "Look at him, he's getting his first screenplay turned into a TV show and now thinks he can talk shit."

Sebastian's show about a group of queer men living, loving, and dating in Los Angeles would go into production sometime in the new year. I couldn't wait to see what he did with it. "All I know is, if there's not a fine Black bartender, we're gonna have words, me and you." I pointed between myself and Sebastian, earning myself a laugh from everyone.

"You mean this fine Black bartender?" Marcus wrapped his arms around me and nuzzled my neck from behind. I trembled because my man was hot and he could get me hot with a simple touch.

Sometimes I still couldn't believe Marcus had chosen me. The weird part? There were times he wondered why I had chosen him. I figured that meant it was human nature. We never saw ourselves as good enough for the people we loved. I was going to work on changing that.

"All *I* know is, if there's a romantic with bad luck with men who has shitty dates, we're gonna have words," Parker joked.

"Even if he gets a sexy husband who loves to tell him what a good boy he is?" Elliott asked in a voice that was all sex. Parker was a lucky man, no doubt about that. Not as lucky as me, though.

"Gross," Declan teased.

Parker basically melted. "Best husband ever."

"Thank you, beautiful." Elliott kissed him.

"Anyone else turned on?" Corbin provided the comic

relief, as usual, and we all laughed again.

He seemed to be doing okay with the fact that his three best friends had fallen in love. Nothing had changed for the Beach Bums when it came to their relationships with each other. They would always be best friends and brothers, and now Corbin had three new people who loved him exactly the way he was. Still, I hoped he'd find someone soon too. He deserved to be loved in all the ways possible.

As if reading my mind, Corbin said, "So...I made a decision I should probably share." He paused for effect. "I'm gonna get myself one of these." He pointed to us.

"One of what? I'm confused," Marcus said.

"A boyfriend. I'm gonna find one."

"Did you try the Boyfriend Warehouse downtown?" Declan asked.

"Ha-ha." Corbin gave him the finger. "I'm serious. I want to try the boyfriend thing too. Anyone have recommendations on where I can get one?"

"You can always marry a guy in Vegas." Parker smiled.

"Nah, that's already been done."

"Worked out well for us." Elliott shrugged.

"Date a movie star who isn't acting?" Sebastian asked.

"Again with the already-been-done. You guys are no help at all."

"What the hell is wrong with you, kid?" Marcus stepped away from me to wrap an arm around Corbin and kiss his temple. Their friendship was so beautiful and one of my favorite things about the man I loved.

"Strange, right? The hard part is how I'm going to deal with missing all the sex."

"Um...why would you have to miss sex? Marcus and I fuck all the time." My boyfriend rolled his eyes at my statement. "What? It's true. And from what I've heard, my boss is a dirty-talking sex machine, while Elliott's over there praising Parker and almost making *me* weak in the knees."

"Yes, but it's okay if you don't have that much sex too," Parker added. "Sex doesn't define a relationship."

"Of course. I'm sex positive *and* positive about people's desires or choices."

"You guys realize we're at a fundraiser?" Declan asked.

We chatted for a while longer, but I kept noticing Corbin's gaze searching the room. I almost asked him if he was planning on finding his boyfriend here, but I didn't want to give him too much shit in case he was serious. According to Marcus, Corbin had always been against settling down in a monogamous relationship, but then all the guys except Parker had been, and look at them now.

"Ugh. Spencer's here," Corbin said.

"The asshole neighbor?" Marcus went into Daddy-mode, looking around the room.

"I hate him, and I don't even know him," Parker added.

Corbin said, "I'm gonna go talk to him. I've made it my mission to annoy the shit out of him."

I looked in the direction he was and saw a fuller-figured guy in a suit. He had neatly styled hair and his arms were crossed. He looked sexy, confident—and was watching Corbin.

When Corbin headed his way, Declan was the first to follow, then Marcus, Parker, and us poddies—which I'd totally started calling us, much to Elliott's dismay.

"Can I help you?" Asshole Spencer said when we approached. I mean, it was probably us who looked like the assholes in this scenario—Corbin's crew coming after him or something.

"Came to say hi. I'm just being polite. You should try it sometime," Corbin replied, and I saw the blaze of fire in

Spencer's eyes.

"I'm not playing this game with you," Asshole Spencer replied.

"Oh, Spencer! Have you met my son?" Cat said, approaching us, so clearly, she knew him. He smiled at her in a way he hadn't with Corbin, but I was pretty sure the look he'd turned on our friend was part annoyance, part I-want-to-jump-your-bones. Cat introduced us, then said, "Spencer is the outreach coordinator for the LGBTQ center here. He's also very active in his work on ending the stigma of HIV and AIDS."

Okay, so maybe Asshole Spencer wasn't an asshole after all.

We all grumbled a nice-to-meet-you because we wanted to have Corbin's back but also had to acknowledge that Spencer did good work.

"Wow. That's really impressive. I'd love to hear more," Corbin said, turning on the charm, which seemed to annoy Spencer but made Cat beam.

"I'm sure you have other things to do," Spencer replied.

"Nope. Not at all. Unless there's some reason you don't want to tell me about your work?"

Spencer gave Corbin a tight smile. "Of course not."

"Great! Come with me. I'll get us a drink," Corbin said, and Spencer reluctantly followed.

Cat went to talk to someone else, and the second she was gone, Elliott asked, "What just happened?"

"I'm not sure," Sebastian said, "but I think Corbin wants to hang out with that Spencer guy."

"I thought Corbin hated him?" Parker questioned.

"You used to think you hated me too, beautiful, and now you're my perfect boy." Elliott winked.

"Um...can I be your perfect boy tonight?" I asked Marcus, who chuckled and pulled me into his arms. It was nice and comfy there.

"Always," he replied.

The guys did some bidding on auction items, and we listened to some of the guest speakers before Corbin made his way back to us.

"Is Asshole Spencer your boyfriend prospect?" I asked him.

"What? No. Why would you ask that?" Corbin's brows pulled together as if he was truly perplexed. Maybe I'd read the room wrong. "I just like annoying him. At first he used to get under my skin, but I've managed to turn the tables on him."

"Just make sure you're not trying to prove something to yourself," Marcus warned. "You don't need his approval."

Corbin rolled his eyes. "Totally not what this is."

Marcus nodded, as did the rest of the guys. We all hung out a little longer before leaving for the night.

"Are we still meeting up with your parents tomorrow?" I asked Marcus in the car ride home. They'd been better about spending time with him. We had dinner once a week, and they hadn't canceled once. Seeing how much they'd hurt their son must've flipped a switch. They'd even decided not to open the new branch. Life was short. Money was great, but family was what mattered.

"Yep. And your family is still coming next week?"

"Yeah, I gotta figure out what to make for them." I was excited to cook for my folks at our house. I was getting prepped for next month when I would start school.

The second we got home, Bossy Marcus took over, ordering me to strip naked, which I gladly did. He fucked me against the door in the entryway, breeding me the way we both loved before we went upstairs and got into the hot tub. I sat between his legs, my back against his chest, Marcus's arms around me as we looked up at the stars.

"That night you got me the telescope? I knew right then my life would never be the same." He kissed my neck.

"Tell me more, baby."

Marcus chuckled. "I love you, Kai."

I smiled. Those words would never get old, and Marcus was better at saying them than he realized. "I love you too, and I will always choose you."

I turned in his arms, wrapped mine around him, and kissed him, my recovering realist when it came to love, at least when we were talking about me.

Want more from *The Vers* crew? Grab Corbin's story, The Charmer!

Find Riley:

Newsletter

Reader's Group
facebook.com/groups/RileysRebels2.0

Facebook
facebook.com/rileyhartwrites

Twitter
twitter.com/RileyHart5

Goodreads
goodreads.com/author/show/7013384.Riley_Hart

Instagram
instagram.com/rileyhartwrites

BookBub
bookbub.com/profile/riley-hart

Other Books by Riley Hart

Series by Riley Hart
Inevitable
Secrets Kept
Briar County
Atlanta Lightning
Blackcreek
Boys In Makeup with Christina Lee
Broken Pieces
Crossroads
Fever Falls with Devon McCormack
Finding
Forbidden Love with Christina Lee
Havenwood
Jared and Kieran
Last Chance
Metropolis with Devon McCormack
Rock Solid Construction
Saint and Lucky
Stumbling Into Love
Wild side

Standalone books:
Boyfriend Goals
Strings Attached
Beautiful & Terrible Things
Love Always
Endless Stretch Of Blue

Looking For Trouble
His Truth

Standalone books with Devon McCormack:
No Good Mitchell
Beautiful Chaos
Weight Of The World
Up For The Challenge

Standalone books with Christina Lee:
Science & Jockstraps
Of Sunlight and Stardust

About the Author

Riley Hart's love of all things romance shines brightly in everything she writes. Her primary focus is Male/Male romance but under various pen names, her prose has touched practically every part of the spectrum of love and relationships. The common theme that ties them all together is stories told from the heart.

A hopeless romantic herself, Riley is a lover of character-driven plots, many with flawed and relatable characters. She strives to create stories that readers can not only fall in love with, but also see themselves in. Real characters and real love blended together equal the ultimate Riley Hart experience.

When Riley isn't creating her next story, you can find her reading, traveling, or dreaming about reading or traveling, and spending time with her two perfectly snarky kids, and one swoon-inducing husband.

Riley Hart is represented by Jane Dystel at Dystel, Goderich & Bourret Literary Management. She's a 2019 Lambda Literary Award Finalist for *Of Sunlight and Stardust*.

Printed in Great Britain
by Amazon